The
Boarding House

MITT YELRUB

PAGE PUBLISHING
Conneaut Lake, PA

First originally published by Page Publishing 2022

ISBN 979-8-88654-692-7 (pbk)
ISBN 979-8-88654-709-2 (digital)

Printed in the United States of America

To Billy Brazill, who inspired me to write. Remember Bobo?
To my brothers Mike and Dan, who are the best storytellers I know.

Contents

The Boarding House 1
Christmas 8
Shopping 15
Timmy 20
Heisenberg 26
Fishing with Jim and Larry 33
Forrest Gump 48
Partaking 54
Buck and Dot 63
Matilda's Christmas 69
Eternity 75
Haunting 79

The Boarding House

If you ever drove by on Main Street, along the US Route that was the other name for Main Street, and saw some folk sitting on the porch or talking to passersby on the sidewalk, you might have wondered what they were saying. If you happen to be one who sits on porches or was once a passerby who stopped for a word, then you may be feeling something familiar. As these tellings progress, you may be able to guess where the place is, but it won't matter much, as only some of what is told is true, the greatest truth being that there is no story worth telling that cannot be improved upon.

I own and run, or I should say, my wife owns and runs a boarding house. I can make a more legitimate claim to ownership than management; at least I have a deed that establishes the fact of ownership, but there is little that provides testimony to any form of management on my part. A boarding house is a somewhat archaic name for what is more commonly referred to as a bed-and-breakfast. But I prefer boarding house, as from time to time, we have lodgers who stay for extended periods of time. Some because they come to work on some project in or near town for several weeks or months, some for reasons no one can say. We do not particularly care as long as they pay the rent and cause no discomfort for me, my wife, and other guests, such as they come and go in the ordinary course.

When I am not occupied with boarding house management, I often can be found in one of the several establishments that are also on Main Street or a tributary street or avenue that runs into Main. Now a thing to bear in mind is that this is a small town, probably not more than five thousand good people who make up year-round residents. We are about forty miles from the nearest city traveling either east or west on the interstate that passes by our town. We have an exit on the interstate, and that is used mostly by the students who come and go to attend the college we have in town. The college students account for another approximately seven thousand people, mostly good, but rarely resident year-round. It also accounts for much of what comprises the rest of Main Street, which includes thirteen bars (some with restaurants), two liquor stores, a pharmacy, a police department, a fire department, a few small grocery stores (one with a gas station), and I imagine, a few lawyers. The hospital and most of the doctors are in the next town over, though a few of the doctors live in town.

Main Street is bisected at the center of town, and our boarding house is on the East Main side of town, number 78. As suggested by this small number, we are within easy walking distance of downtown and all that it has to offer. We have a beautiful creek that runs through town on its route to one of the inland seas called the Great Lakes. This is another site for me to pass time, fishing the creek. It is about three miles as the crow flies from town to the lake but a good seven miles if you walk it. The creek and the fishing to be found on it and on the lake is another reason we have visitors, mostly bed-and-breakfast types, in our town. Inasmuch as I share an interest in fishing and know the seven miles of that walk to the lake, we attract a disproportionate number of guests, particularly when the steelhead are running.

That number, however, rarely exceeds five, the number of rooms we have to let. The house has six rooms and five bathrooms if you include the one occupied by me and my wife. We can stretch the number of guests to eight if one was willing to share a room, as three of the rooms, each of these with their own bath, have two beds. The other two rooms hold a king-size bed but share a bathroom, Jack-and-Jill style. So if couples are in each of those, I reckon a full house will be ten guests. My wife and I make twelve. We do not have any children at home but do keep a dog, an orange-and-white Brittany, that, except in the winter, sleeps on the porch and a cat who sleeps in the barn at all times. At least we think she does; she was spayed, so we don't know if she is sleeping around, but she is useful for keeping the mouse population down. The dog—despite my prowess as a hunter, which I do when I'm not fishing or visiting our downtown businesses—does little to keep the local pheasant and grouse population down. At best, I suppose she drives them out of our county, as I seldom see her hunting in front of me. Good thing they call it fishing and hunting and not catching and shooting; even better, none of our guests are dependent upon my outdoor ventures for the board or breakfast aspects of our offering.

Now despite our small number, and as already referred to in the context of the cat's domicile, we do have a barn; we also have a bit of woods behind the house that back up to the Pioneer Cemetery. Like most cemeteries in town, the Pioneer is smallish, comprising about three acres, and has no one in it who was buried in the last one hundred years. What is nice about this setup is that while lots on Main Street are not very deep, or very wide for that matter, from number 50 to the end of the block heading east, there are about a dozen homes that have nothing behind them but woods and beyond that cemetery. The boarding house itself is a historic property, dating from around 1830; it was originally owned by the Baptist church and served as the residence for the church's minister and family. Some folk still refer to it as the parsonage for that reason. We are only the second owners, having acquired from the church after nearly 150 years in that service.

I am not sure why we acquired the property, but there was something that attracted us to it. I mentioned we have no children at home, but we do have six who are out of the house, some with homes and children of their own. I guess we figured that with all those rooms, they would come to visit. Well, if they do, they will have to call ahead so we can keep some rooms open for them. They are, of course, always welcome, no charge. In case they are wondering which house, it is the two-tone brown (light on the bottom clapboard, dark on the top cedar shakes) house at 78 East Main Street. On the ground floor, there is a foyer with a staircase on the left that leads to the upper rooms. The walls in the foyer are white, as is the woodwork. Not very imaginative, but there is an old oak parquet floor in its natural color, and the banister to the stair and the stair treads are the original black walnut, which is oiled and polished to a brilliance. A brilliance that reflects a bright chandelier that illuminates the foyer and stair that opens to a loft on the second floor with about the same footprint as the foyer. Big enough to form a small sitting area for the guests.

To the right of the foyer, you pass through a double-pocket door into a parlor that can comfortably seat ten or so. Besides the furniture for ten, the room also has a fireplace, which is one of my chores to keep ready for burning and burning if burning. There is also an upright piano, a Baldwin that was owned by my wife's mother for a while. Now the mother of my wife is still living, so I was a bit dubious as to how or why we ended up with the piano. My wife does play; though not enough to please me, she plays quite well. But other than occasional tuning, the piano seems to be in good order, so I guess my suspicions were unwarranted. Besides my wife, it seems more than a few of our guests had lessons in their lives and, for some reason, are inclined to sit down and practice when visiting. Whether it is chopsticks or Chopin, the pleasure they take from playing is satisfying enough for me; the playing, at various times, can mitigate or ameliorate that pleasure. The windows along the front of the parlor face onto the porch.

Behind the foyer and parlor, there is a dining room that you enter through an archway that leads from the parlor. We keep it set up with two tables that can seat four (they can be joined to accommodate a larger party) and three tables that can seat two, though these are typically occupied solo. Everyone gets served breakfast—that's the bed-and-breakfast part—for our boarders, and for those who arrange it, we also prepare dinner. My wife and I need to eat anyhow, and she is used to cooking for eight people as it is, so this is no real additional effort. It keeps me from having to eat too many leftovers, as she is having a challenging time cooking for a smaller number. Everything is family-style, and there is no menu in the sense of things to choose from. We set up a menu at the beginning of the week; and boarders, when we have them, get to express preferences for meals they favor or fancy.

Just to the right of the dining room is a room, about half the width of the dining room, that I have set up as a bar. We don't have a liquor license, so I cannot charge for any alcohol dispensed. But I do keep a small supply; as I am inclined, from time to time, to drink a glass of Jameson, neat, which, when in a convivial mood, I have been known to share with just about anyone who happens to be near. If someone prefers other spirits, wines, or beers, recall that downtown is a short walk and served by no less than two liquor stores. Competition keeps the prices fair. If you are a repeat customer, we have been known to make room in the liquor cabinet for you, and we have a few locals who come off the porch from time to time who avail themselves of this service. Good thing too, I am neither convivial nor wealthy enough to consistently share with this group, though we do well enough accommodating one another's company. My wife does not permit smoking; I am not a huge fan of it, though I may allow myself an occasional cigar. But those so inclined can head to the porch.

Behind the dining room is the kitchen. There's not much time spent there by me, so I am having a hard time coming up with a description of it. Most of what comes out of it is good; the food is good as often are the scents that precede it. Typically, it is the scent of a meal in preparation that serves to roust all guests in the morning and whet the appetite of those with dinner arrangements. The odors seem to know their way up to the guest rooms or across to the bar where most are found in preparation for their repast. The bar more so for evening meals, though we have had some breakfasts start with Bloody Mary, mimosa, and poinsettia; and from time to time, we have a shift worker who may want a drink coming off the eleven to seven. No license, no rules. I've always found rules hard to enforce anyhow; common sense and courtesy seem to work better.

The remainder of the ground floor comprises the private residence of me and my wife. These rooms lie to the back and right of the kitchen and butt up against the bar. We are pretty humble in our trappings; we sometimes think we have just enough to be left wanting for more. But what we don't have in possessions we have in pleasures that we pluck from the moments we try to live to the fullest. We don't live in the past but prize more than anything our memories, memories that are happy enough to leave us with only positive expectations of what the future holds. Most importantly, we have each other, and my wife pleases me; I hope I do the same for her. Our quarters include a bedroom that is big enough for our king bed, a sofa, a chair, and a table for sitting and where I am writing this. There is a laundry/utility room that allows us to keep our own laundry clean as well as the bed and table linens needed for the house. Of course, there is a bathroom, but the toilet and sink are separated from the rest, as it serves as a small powder room that is just off the back of the bar. We have the only key by which to gain access to the rest of the bathroom. I thought once of taking the powder room out and putting in a fireplace that would serve both the bar and our bedroom, but that would mean I would have to build a new bathroom for our quarters, and that would leave none other on the first floor.

The upstairs contains two levels; the original of the house had only one, but we converted the attic into two bedrooms with the Jack-and-Jill adjoining bathrooms. This also necessitated a new staircase, which, unlike the original, was made of white pine and covered by a runner. The stair ran to the center of the attic from the top of which you could turn right and then right again to enter one bedroom or left to enter the other. The bathroom, of course, is between the two rooms. These rooms are of no distinctive character in the historical sense of the house since they are of recent vintage and essentially new construction; this was not only of value in respect of the bathroom and related plumbing but also enabled a somewhat modern amenity of a little wet bar, essentially a sink with a small refrigerator tucked below in each room. These rooms are covered wall to wall with carpeting that reflected the period of their construction but conveyed nothing of the history or feel of the main house.

On the second floor, there are three bedrooms, each with their own baths and toilets, admittedly of recent addition but kept in character of the period of the original house that is the true charm to which most visitors are attracted or commented on in departing. I am not sure why because most of what happens in these rooms is sleeping, but with sleeping comes dreaming, and perhaps the sense of the rooms set the context for dreams and historical places carry a certain amount of nostalgia, imagined and real, that may fuel some good dreams. We had more than one guest who insisted that the rooms are haunted, and on that, we will have more to tell. Indeed, and sadly, we have had more than one guest pass away in these rooms, but again I anticipate tellings to come. All the rooms have their original wood floors that are covered with various patterned area rugs that match the color and decor schemes devised by my wife. All the furniture is genuine antique but from different eras spanning the full epoch of the house. My brother's wife assisted in the antiquing of the house. She has a black belt in antiquing and shopping in general. My brother defines an antique as something his wife bought thirty years ago and after full use threw out and in another seventy years someone will buy again. His point being that we are now buying things people used for thirty years and threw out seventy or more years ago.

Anyhow, over the years, we have had many people visit the house, bed-and-breakfasters and boarders. Each has given us a certain amount of pleasure for their uniqueness, and some have been quite remarkable, making deep impressions on our memories. Memories that are the source of some tellings, and as I said before, any story worth telling is worth improving upon.

Christmas

Most of us are familiar with the butterfly effect. That's the theory that says when a butterfly flaps its wings, the turbulence that arises sets in motion a series of cascading events that can lead to rather significant outcomes.

I forget what year it was, but it was a year that the three rooms on the second floor had been occupied for most of the summer and autumn by boarders. Two of the fellows, Jim and Dave, had been there since the first of July, working on a natural gas well that was being drilled. Interestingly, our town had been the site of the first natural gas well in the United States, and I guess we had not pumped all the gas out because someone had found more, and here were these two fellows to work on drilling wells.

While Jim and Dave worked for the same company, prior to coming here, they did not know each other. Jim was an engineer, while Dave seemed to know everything Jim did; they were able to talk to each other without as much confusion as they caused me. Dave apparently did not have the same degrees as Jim and was considerably more sullied than Jim at the end of the day. Dave had the dirt ground permanently into his rough hands and under his nails—so much so no matter how much he scrubbed, it never came out. His arms were thicker, and even his elbows were calloused. Based on their own tellings, I reckoned Dave learned most of what he knew from his time in the military. I thought he might have been in the Army, but I wasn't sure because he talked a lot about being at sea and the CBs, which I thought were the radios that truckers used and, for some time, were popular among us common folk for use in our cars.

I never had much use for a CB, mostly because I could not afford one. I guess more so because I never saw a great-enough need to afford one. However, I recall one night sitting in the bar when Walt—one of the locals who never spent a night in the house, if you don't count the times he slept on the porch—insisted that the CB was the best thing since sliced beer. He thought everyone should have one, and his primary argument was that it would be particularly important for the defense of the nation. Walt had the uncanny ability to see things in an expansive way, which led him to conceive of all sorts of threats and opportunities that most of us did not consider. Walt felt the CB would save us all when we came under attack because it would enable us to communicate the position of the enemy. Walt spent some time in the military a couple of years after high school and did a lot of recon in Vietnam, so he was particularly concerned about enemy positions and communicating them. These days, Walt manages the truck stop out by the interstate—another critical mission related to our national fuel supply.

Anyhow, both Jim and Dave were fine fellows and easy to be with. They both worked hard, but when they had some downtime, they played just as hard. I took them fishing a couple of times on the creek, and more than once, they were up for the full seven-mile walk. Neither of them favored fly-fishing as I did. Both used worms, sinkers, and bobbers and, truthfully, caught more fish than me; though most of them were suckers that they could have caught on a kernel of corn. During these times, we all got to know one another pretty well and passed some easy conversation among us. I learned that Jim was married once but had spent quite a bit of time out of the country in places like Saudi Arabia and Kuwait, mostly drilling for oil. Neither of these places was very hospitable to women, so his wife did not travel with him. While Jim got to scratch his itch for travel and adventure, being away from his wife left her with a few itches of her own that weren't getting scratched. Eventually, these situations were not hospitable to married life, and Jim's wife found another pole to back up against to scratch her itches.

Dave, on the other hand, had done most of his international travel with the military. He had been to a lot of places, none for too long but enough to have plenty of stories. You had to pull the stories out of Dave, as he made them somewhat reluctantly. It's hard to say why, and I reckon it doesn't much matter. But I am not sure if it was his private nature, a reluctance to share, or that he did not think his telling was as interesting as it ultimately was for the listening. When you could get them out of him, Dave had some of the best stories I ever heard. Dave was, and still is, married. He would phone his wife every night, and at least once every month, sometimes twice, he would travel home to see her. I reckon they knew how to scratch each other's itches and kept it together in the doing—well enough to have two children, a boy and a girl, in that order. You could sure see the joy in his face when he spoke of his family, and in that regard, it was no problem to get him to do so.

Jim and Dave, as boarders, were often around in the evening and had become regulars with Walt, Cosmo, and Tad who were locals who used our liquor cabinet. We all got along well until a new boarder, Eli, moved into the house that September. As any new element introduced into a sensitive ecosystem can set things off, or at least in a new direction, at first, we weren't sure of Eli. He was a gregarious guy and had no trouble fitting in at a certain level. Eli had a strong personality and was instantly likeable, but the rest of us— Jim, Dave, and the locals—already had some common experiences that we had shared both in doing and telling that, well, Eli just was not a part of yet.

Eli was here to work on a project at the college, something that seemed foreign to us, and he was not sure if it would be weeks or months. Like I said, we all got along, and slowly Eli worked his way into the tribe we had formed. He earned his feathers, though, when the early steelhead season started. First, impressing me, he took right to fly-fishing, and there was no looking back. Moreover, he caught more than any of us that season and one that was a real trophy, which among favorably disposed males is enough to charter your member-ship in whatever ad hoc society we males are prone to form.

It was that December when Eli was traveling; this was not unusual as he often traveled for a couple of days at a time during which he kept his room at the house. On December 23, I received a call from Eli, not sure where he was calling from, but he was asking what size of sweater I thought Dave would wear. I told him I wasn't sure but would guess that he was a large; I also offered that I had his wife's phone number and he could ask her. He said no; it was just that he was at Cabela's, and he recalled Dave being cold and thought he would get him a sweater for Christmas.

Well, I no doubt contributed to what ensued. That night at the bar, Dave and Jim were present, as were Cosmo, Walt, and Tad; and the general topic of Christmas shopping came up. We were all in various stages of completion of this annual task, and then I mentioned the call I got from Eli. Dave mumbled, "Shit!" I asked, "What's wrong?" And he proceeded to explain he had never thought of getting any of us Christmas gifts or one for Eli but if Eli was buying a gift for him, he would now have to reciprocate. Then Walt expanded that into speculation that if Eli were buying a gift for Dave, he might not be planning on stopping there and would likely include me and Jim, not to mention himself, Cosmo, and Tad whose society he now kept. We locals would naturally be here for Christmas; Jim's plans included staying as well. Dave, of course, would return to his family to spend Christmas with them, but that did not get him off the hook of reciprocation. We agreed to meet the next morning to remedy the situation and agreed to reassemble the next night in the bar to exchange gifts, absent Dave who would be leaving that afternoon for home.

Eli was due to arrive around 4:00 p.m. on December 24, and Dave had departed at noon the same day. I had built a fire in the fireplace in the parlor. We had the Christmas tree set up there as well. The warm glow of the fire mixed with the lights of the tree as the smoky scent of the fire mingled with the scent of the tree and the turkey roasting in the oven. The days being shorter this time of year, it was already turning dark when Eli arrived to be greeted by this cocktail of glowing color and mingled scents. Truthfully, it was absolutely delicious. Eli greeted Jim and me and said he was going to his room to get settled before dinner, commenting on how good it smelled and how hungry he was. We told him to meet us in the bar and that we would have a drink before dining. He said he would be right down. In the meantime, Tad then Walt and Cosmo arrived, all bearing gifts like the three wise men of the Bible.

When Eli descended the stairs and walked from the parlor, he saw my wife setting the tables, which were brought together for all of us. Turning into the bar, he saw the whole crew assembled and was startled to see us all, but we raised our glasses in cheer and offered him a fresh pour with which to join us. Then full of the silly pride of one-upmanship, we announced our intention to do a Christmas gift exchange. We, of course, had bought one another token gifts, agreeing not to spend more than $5 on each; but gauging what a sweater at Cabela's might cost, we had each spent around $50 on our gifts for Eli, figuring that would be his benchmark. Eli looked at us, all beaming, beaming right back and explaining that it was his tradition to give gifts on Christmas morning. Reckoning that we had taken him by surprise and not left him time to do the wrapping, we all figured it would be best to proceed, carried on by the conviviality we were experiencing.

We proceeded to exchange gifts, with another round of drinks as each diminished his pile. Truth be told, we had a grand old time. The $5 budget resulted in some pretty humorous gifts that turned out to provide some insight on little quirks we saw in one another. Eli, of course, made out well, and we had so many drinks and laughs that all the awkwardness of the situation, what with Eli not dispensing anything, passed comfortably. Moreover, it left us all with the anticipation of what would greet us in the morning. My wife came in just as we were handing out the last of Dave's gifts, in absentia, calling us to dinner and leaving no loose ends.

The meal was extraordinary. My wife is a good cook, but it was made even more extraordinary by the cheerfulness and good feelings that had been engendered with our earlier proceedings. Tad and Cosmo couldn't stay for dinner; they had families of their own that had some expectation they would spend Christmas Eve with them. Tad had a wife. Of course, she was always welcome; but for some reason, she seldom came along. And when she did, it tended to alter the mood—not in a bad way, just altered—when we were all together. Even my wife steered clear of the numerous ad hoc men's societies that would erupt at intervals in the bar. Cosmo, or Cos, was a widower and had a son from that marriage. His son was in high school and was of the age when you don't spend a lot of time with Dad, but it was Christmas. Walt was a bachelor and had only to go up to the filling station at eleven to change over shifts. The station was open 24-7. So Walt joined us. Dinner broke up around ten thirty or so, and we all went to bed wishing one another a Merry Christmas.

The next morning came, and I did not emerge from my residence into the kitchen until about nine thirty. Walt, Tad, and Cosmo were already there and assembled in the bar. My wife had made a pot of coffee and had served them, so I grabbed a cup and went in to see what Santa had brought everyone. Most importantly, we were all anticipating continuing the momentum that was started the evening before with our gift exchange capped off by the grand finale of Eli's dispensing. Jim ambled down shortly after me; I am not sure if it was the noise or the smell of the coffee that got his attention. But we were all assembled with a level of excitement and anticipation, waiting for Eli Claus to arrive.

As it approached 10:00 a.m., and some of us on our second and third cups of coffee, there was still no Eli. I got up and walked to the kitchen and asked my wife if she had seen Eli this morning. She said, "Yes." Satisfied, I wheeled around and headed back to the bar/breakfast nook but was brought to a stop as she continued, "He was up about six thirty this morning. He loaded his car, had some toast and coffee, and told me he was off to his next assignment." She added, "He paid up through today." I was dumbstruck; a flood of confusing and conflicting thoughts entered my head. Did he leave our gifts? Wait, did he give us the old head fake, tricking us into the whole gift exchange with that innocuous phone call? Oh shit, did we talk ourselves into this whole thing and embarrass the guy into leaving because he did not have anything for us? He was probably wondering why we would arrange a gift exchange and not tell him about it.

Well, anyhow, that phone call about Dave's sweater size was the flutter of the butterfly's wing that set in motion a series of events that, in the end, turned out well for everyone. When I returned to the bar to update everyone on Eli, I also ran through my thinking on the whole affair, which was admittedly still a bit confused. Everyone's thinking lined up, at least initially, with one or the other of my thoughts. Of course, Walt had his own spin on things; but in the end, we all agreed it did not much matter. We had a fun time with our gift exchange; Walt, Tad, Cosmo, and I continue it to this day. The budget is still $5, and the gifts are still mostly humorous. We figured if we somehow offended Eli, we had made up for it by the nice gifts he got from all of us. And in any event, he must not have been too offended; while we have never crossed paths again, he sends a Christmas card every year with no mention of the gift exchange.

Shopping

We have all had a bittersweet experience that combines conflicting feelings. A lot of the important things in life are like this. For example, when your kid graduates from school, the cocktail made with pride and joy extracted from their accomplishment is often mixed with a touch of loss from the sense that this is just another step away from you. Both feelings can make you cry, and it is hard to say which caused the tears. Not that it really matters because you end up looking silly blubbering in front of all those people. Well, there was one such instance when I was raging with jealousy, furious with incredulity, and lusting to make love because of my wife.

It was a spring morning. One of those days where you knew it was going to be nice, but for the first part of the morning, it was still a bit fresh with the coolness in the air. When I woke up—it was about seven thirty—my wife was gone from her usual place next to me in bed. While I lay there gathering my senses and mentally organizing my day, I heard the back door slamming shut and some rustling around in the kitchen. So I figured she must have gone out to do some grocery shopping and was in the process of putting things away. She liked to do this sometimes—to get the shopping out of the way before the stores got crowded.

Anyhow, I slipped on a pair of gray sweatpants—I usually sleep au naturel—and headed out to the kitchen to get my first cup of coffee before I showered and dressed. When I walked into the kitchen, my speculation was confirmed; there was the wife reaching up, on tiptoes, shoving a bag of flour onto the top shelf of the pantry cupboard. She still had her coat on, a light-green trench coat that came just below the knee and was cinched around her waist with a belt. She was wearing her flats, a black ballet slipper-like shoe with a real thin sole. At first, I didn't think anything of it, it being—as noted—a brisk spring morning. So I offered to take her coat so she could keep at storing her wares.

That was when I got the first sense of conflicting feelings. She spun around from the cupboard with a little hop at the end of her turn that caused her auburn hair to spring up then down, coming to rest just on top of her shoulders. She wore a sheepish, shy smile, but a clear look of mischief shot from her hazel eyes. She loosened the belt, unbuttoned the buttons, her smile growing wider to show her perfect teeth, and let the coat drop to the floor. Now it turned out that besides the flats, her smile was the only thing she was wearing.

"What the hell?" was the best I could muster as a response. If she ever decides to write a book, I will let her describe how I looked. How I was feeling only I know for sure, and this was surely one of those bittersweet moments. My first thoughts and feelings were completely natural because that's the way I am. Now mind you, my wife has rounded the corner on fifty, as have I, and has birthed six children, all of which are adults today; but she still has a body that, as the song goes, is a wonderland. She's not tall, and she's not small. She is petite but voluptuous in her breasts and hips, "tits and ass" as another song goes, that blossom from her tiny waist. Her breasts mimicked the slight bounce of her hair but were still firm enough to come to a rest after the first hop. They hung there, full as a drop of water that accumulates at the end of a leaf at its most heavy point just before breaking away and dropping. It was as if her erect nipples, pointing perkily with a slight upward bend, were attached by invisible string to the ceiling, or the stars, holding her pendulous breasts in place. Still smiling, she bent forward, creating a slow, slight separation of her breasts from her rib cage, to grab a jug of milk from the sac; rose back into an upright position, giving her shoulders a slight backward thrust, again a gentle, firm jiggle; and walked past me. My eyes were locked on her as she walked by me toward the refrigerator, her narrow waist expanding out to her wide hips that carried her buxom butt cheeks that were dimpled and had, too, a slight but firm jiggle as she stepped. And then as she grabbed the door handle and bent over to put the milk in the door, her butt took the perfect shape, like the top half of an hourglass from her waist around her hips narrowing again at her thighs, with a fuzzy little flower blossoming where the sand runs through to the next level.

All this occurred within seconds; I was dumbstruck and simultaneously enraged thinking my wife went into public like this or was so thinly veiled from being in public like this. I was also insanely jealous thinking that the public could share in this experience of my wife. "What the hell" was again the only response I had. Well, at least verbally. She seemed to be prolonging the task of getting that milk jug into the door, and as the shock wore off, I noted that my sweatpants had become a little tight on my ass and I had pitched a tent below my belly button. She returned to a full standing position; turned around, pushing the door shut behind her; and still smiling, took notice of the effect she had on me. She then walked toward me, reached into the tent, and helped me to take it down by repositioning the pole, saying, "Let's see if we can take care of that."

Well, we retreated to our chambers, and the rest of that morning is not for telling. We had no boarders or guests at the time, so we ended up having a late breakfast. This also gave me plenty of time to work through the conflicting and bittersweet feelings by which I was at first overwhelmed. And somehow, I was reminded of how very often my wife could smile through my difficulties and always managed, in the end, to bring out the best in me.

There's an intimacy between lovers that occurs in sex. It's not the only time we feel love, but it certainly is among the more intense. This is not news to most folk; even Solomon wrote about in the Song of Songs, and that made it to the Bible. He uses the intensity of these feelings of love to express the love God feels for us, which got me to thinking about what Izaak Walton said in *The Compleat Angler* pondering the beauty of nature: "If God provides this for one as unworthy as me, imagine what he has in store for his angels and the saints in heaven," or something along those lines. I haven't read many books, but I have read these two, and I find it interesting how these are somehow connected.

While still pondering such things, I decided I would go fishing. Since it was already midmorning, though we had just finished our late breakfast, I decided to make a sandwich to take along. I noticed a near three-foot-long French baguette still in one of the sacs the wife brought home from her shopping adventure. I genuinely enjoy this style of bread, crunchy crust on the outside and chewy white meat on the inside. I am not sure what the proper term is, and most people make sandwiches by putting real meat on the inside. But in my case, I was going to put some cheese and mustard in my sandwich. I sawed off about a third of the loaf, cut it laterally in half, and layered in one level of Swiss cheese with a slight overlap from slice to slice. I don't like my sandwiches too thick. I was in Manhattan once and ordered a sandwich at a deli; they put more meat on that one sandwich than the wife normally buys for a week at the grocery store. I could only eat about half of it. After that, I took out the squirt bottle of the French's mustard and squiggled on a thin ribbon in one direction then turned around in the other, making figure 8s. This was the perfect cheese sandwich: the crunch of the crust, the soft meaty dough of the bread, the substantial creaminess of the cheese, and the slight pique of spice and bitter of the mustard. I could taste it without taking a bite. I wrapped it in foil, put it in the back of my fishing vest, grabbed my rod and reel, and headed off to the creek.

I don't have to walk far to get to the creek, as it runs right through the middle of town; it darn near separates East and West Main Street. Nearly, it is actually on the West Main side of town. But the best place to enter is behind the old primary school on Eagle Street. Behind the school, there is a playground and a Little League Baseball field. You have to walk through the playground, hop a chain-link fence, and then bushwhack, about fifty yards, to the stream. The primary reason to start here is because it is a little more difficult to access, which means fewer people go there, and there is a nice fishing hole there. Otherwise, you can just enter in town by the fire hall.

I fished that hole for about an hour and caught a few rainbow trout, as well as a few creek chub. I am primarily a fly fisherman and seldom keep what I catch. What I like best about fishing is the solitude, the walk along and in the stream, and what happens when you connect with a fish. There's just something about the poetry of the motion to cast a fly out in front of you. If done properly, it lands gently in the water and surrenders itself to the motion of the stream. If you're lucky, the water will present your fly as an appetizer, a course, or maybe a whole meal to a fish. Fish will strike in different ways, but my favorite with a dry fly on is to watch the fish slowly rise and open its mouth, creating a little pillow where the water moves around the fish and an eddy where it completes the circle on the other side as the fish sucks in your fly. That's when the calmness ends. With a little tug, perfectly timed, you set your hook, and the fish reacts. That fish is going to fight and do everything in its power to separate, and you are trying to stay connected, ironically by the thinnest line and tippet you feel you can tie on. During that time, you feel that fish, you are connected to it, and you really get lost in the water, the movement, and your connection with it all. It is truly a Zen-like, mystical moment.

I was fortunate enough to have several of those moments at that hole, but I think the fish got wise, as after four hookups, those fish were staying glued to the bottom. I tied on some weighted streamers and tried those for a while, but I guess when eating starts to hurt and your belly isn't getting filled, even a fish is smart enough to stop. I headed north on the stream to fish some other holes. I crossed under the bridges at Water Street, West Main Street, and Risley Avenue and eventually arrived at the last hole of the day. I connected with a few more fish over the next three hours and felt nicely fatigued and remembered my cheese sandwich. I got out of the water, broke down my rod and reel, and put them in my vest. I took out my sandwich and enjoyed it, now actualizing what I was thinking about earlier. I pondered that if I had added a few slices of ham, I would have a ham-and-cheese sandwich, and I wondered if that spicy-bitter taste of mustard was normal. *Does mustard ever go bad?*

I must have been more fatigued than I thought. It was a busy morning followed by the exertion of wading the stream for about three miles, and I dozed off into a little woods nap.

Timmy

I mentioned there was a dog, specifically an orange-and-white Brittany, with which we kept company. Brittanies are sometimes referred to as Brittany spaniels because they have some physical characteristics in common with other spaniel breeds, like the Welsh or cocker spaniels. Mostly, it is the floppy ears that they have in common with these breeds that give them their kinship. The spaniel designation was dropped along the way since a Brittany displays more of the characteristics of a pointing breed or a bird dog versus a spaniel that is a flushing breed, the former preferring feathers and the latter fur in its hunting predilections. Our dog, Timmy, didn't seem to care much about this distinction or the whole thing about pointing, as he would give chase to just about anything that moved.

When we got him as a puppy, we named him Tim—for no reason. I preferred monosyllabic names because if your dog ran off, it took less energy to walk around yelling one syllable versus two or more. Pete is another good name for this reason. Somehow or other, his name morphed into Timmy, doubling the effort of calling for a lost dog. I think it got started because of my wife; when he was a puppy, before he ran off for the first time, she would talk to the dog like it was a baby, and that included calling him Timmy instead of Tim. This managed to stick, but it doesn't really matter much because the dog doesn't seem to hear when you call him, whatever you call him. He comes and goes as he pleases.

Timmy was, among other things, the source of a small feud between me and my neighbor Mike. In truth, Mike was a pretty good guy, kept his property neat, and except for Timmy, liked animals. He had built a koi pond, which was also home to some ducks he kept, and he had a pet rabbit that was in a cage. Now whenever I got irritated with Mike, I would rail about why some guy would put all that effort into keeping some colorful carp in his yard, with a bunch of noisy shitting birds that did not even lay eggs you could eat, and on top of that, keep a rabbit in a cage that did absolutely nothing. I should note that the only time I became irritated with Mike was when he complained about Timmy going into his yard and splashing in the koi pond while chasing the ducks and trying to do the same to the rabbit that could only hop around the cage. Fortunately, the ducks could fly away, but that poor rabbit must have been insane. Just to keep to the whole truth, the cat showed some interest in the koi once but decided she preferred the much smaller mice that would migrate from the woods behind the house. Mike referred to my animals as the terrorists.

See, that was the big difference between me and Mike, that and that he preferred men to women in a sexual way. I kept animals for a use, Timmy for hunting and Sass for mousing, whereas he was building a zoo with no purpose that you could not meet with a short walk in the woods. It was the latter difference that got to me, creating what the law calls an attractive nuisance for Timmy and then complaining to me about a dog doing what dogs do. Otherwise, Mike and I got along fine.

That was until the one day I came home late in the afternoon and saw a heap of fur lying in the backyard. Timmy was in his usual place on the porch, sleeping, but his muzzle was caked in dirt. I grabbed a stick and walked over to the heap and, to my horror, discovered Mike's rabbit lying there. The animal was clearly deceased, a bit mangled, and had a dirt cake too. I didn't know what to do. I mean, if that rabbit somehow got out of its cage, how could you hold a dog accountable for what is effectively an instinct? I don't care that they dropped spaniel from the breed designation; he still is prone to chase and, apparently, catch fur. So my first reaction was to conceal the evidence by collecting the demised rabbit in a plastic shopping bag and getting it into the barn.

I was in a panic. The wife was not there, so I had no one with which to share the burden of the thoughts that were racing through my head. I went into the house and just sat at the bar. After about an hour or so, I heard Mike returning home as his car pulled into the driveway that separated our homes. His car door shut, and I could hear his footfalls on the steps to his house and the screen door slam behind him as he entered his home. I thought, *Should I put an end to this anguish and go over and tell him? It would probably go easier in the long run if I just came clean.* Another fifteen minutes passed, and again I heard the screen door slap against the frame and the footfalls, this time down the steps. *Shit, too late*, I thought. *Now he is likely about to discover his rabbit missing. It will be hard to explain what it is doing in my barn in a plastic shopping bag.* God, the anxiety and panic in me were mounting. I got up and poured a dram of Jamo and took a sip. *Fuck, this will only make it worse. He'll smell alcohol on my breath and think I committed Oryctolaguscide.* Then it came.

I heard the footsteps on my front porch. The doorbell rang. I swallowed the last of my Jameson, took a deep breath, and walked to the door. It was Walt. I opened the door, and what was brewing in me for the last hour and a half boiled over.

"Walt, what the fuck are you doing ringing the doorbell like that?"

"Like what?"

"You usually just walk in."

"The door isn't usually fucking locked. What's wrong with you?"

I spilled the whole story to Walt. Walt was listening calmly, but the whole time you could see he was thinking on something. He let me finish, and by the time it took and from the telling, I calmed down quite a bit. As usual, and I should have known better, Walt saw a little deeper into things. He started spinning things that could happen to me, especially if the Oryctolaguscide charge could be made to stick. What with bagging the evidence, I was at least an accessory to the crime. It hadn't occurred to me at the time no crime had actually been committed, but it was easy to get caught in the web of Walt's mind. By then, the wife had come home, but we already decided we would keep her innocent by not telling her. Besides, Walt and I had a plan.

Walt decided he would stay for dinner, which was part of the plan. We had a couple of boarding guests who had signed on for dinner; they weren't here long enough to form a new ad hoc society, so they each dined alone, feigning interest in the evening newspaper or some magazine. In truth, being left to ourselves only mounted the intensity of our fervor as cohorts in the next stage of obfuscation. It also lessened the likelihood that someone would cut through the web of Walt's mind and set me free. The wife, Walt, and I ate together; she sensed something was up but had known us both long enough not to ask. She came close though, because I made the mistake of asking her what she did that day and acted interested in the answer. This was something I rarely do and is seldom necessary given her propensity for speech. I know she was tempted to ask me the same.

Anyhow, as nightfall descended, Walt and I made our excuses, claiming we had something that needed working on out in the barn. Walt asked the wife if she could make him a pot of hot water for some tea as a diversion for me to grab shampoo and the blow-dryer and steal it away to the barn. This was all part of the plan. I was in the barn when Walt arrived with his thermos of hot water and a cup with two tea bags. This did not create any suspicion, as Walt was actually a tea drinker. I prefer coffee, but it doesn't matter. We needed the hot water to bathe and shampoo the victim. There were no broken bones and, as far as we could tell, no blood. After the bath, we gave the deceased a blow-dry, fluffed her up nicely, and waited for full darkness to descend. Between the warm bath and the blow-dry, she seemed a little less stiff. Around ten thirty, we completed our mission—I wanted to wait a bit longer, but Walt had to get to the filling station for the eleven shift change—and placed the remains of the rabbit back in her cage.

Walt headed off to the filling station, and I to the house. When I came in, the wife was sitting there in her bathrobe, hair wet, and asked me what we were doing so long in the barn. I told her we had to fix the mower, and then we just got to talking when Walt looked at his watch and had to run for the shift change. She then asked if

I had seen the blow-dryer anywhere and started to declare she was losing her mind, explaining that as she got in the shower, she would have sworn there was a new bottle of shampoo, then she couldn't find the blow-dryer. I just shrugged, said nothing, and went to bed. If she ever does lose her mind, it will likely be because of me; she'll just never know the half of it though.

The first few days weren't bad, though I have to admit I felt a little like a character in a Dostoyevsky novel—convinced everyone who looked at me knew of my guilt and were laying a trap of justice that would snap close upon me. Or like my brother says, "The guy with a hole in his pants walks around thinking everyone can see his ass hanging out, but he is the only one that really knows it's there." I purposely avoided contact with Mike, and as the fifth day rolled around, I started to let other thoughts play in my mind and finally closed the chapter, figuring this too had passed.

The following weekend, we were doing a little grilling in the backyard. Mike must have smelled the chicken on the grill and came out and started walking toward me. It all came back, the world got smaller, and all I could see was Mike striding directly toward me and the grill. My thoughts immediately went to the notion that he suspected me of grilling rabbit. This was all the evidence needed; the jaws of justice were snapping shut. *It's chicken. I swear it's chicken.*

He held out his hand, smiled, and said, "Beautiful day."

"Sure is. Care for a beer?"

"If I say no, I didn't understand the question."

"Well, I have what are no doubt your favorite kinds." He looked at me quizzically. "Free and cold."

I don't know where guys come up with such bullshit and why it always seems funny. "Yes" and "Here" would have done just as well for a guy who adheres to the proverb "Speak less, say more." So I peeled the ring back on a Miller Lite and handed it to him, and we continued our neighborly banter. I was fairly well convinced about halfway through our beers that Mike neither knew nor suspected what had happened with the rabbit.

Then a wry smile broke across his face, and he said, "You know, last week I thought I had witnessed a miracle."

"Oh yeah? What was that?"

"Well, last week, I was going out to feed the koi, and I looked over at the rabbit cage"—a lump formed in my throat, and my heart began to race—"and what I saw shocked the hell out of me."

"What was that?"

"I saw the rabbit lying there in her cage."

"Well, how does that qualify as a miracle?"

"Well, it's the damnedest thing. The rabbit had died the day before. I dug a hole in the yard to bury her that night. I thought I was witnessing a rabbit resurrection. No miracle though. She was as dead as the day before but looked as if she were just born."

"How do you suppose that happened?"

"Don't know. I just buried her again in the same hole. Looked like something dug it up, but still not sure how she got back in her cage."

He swallowed the last of his beer, set down his can, shook his head, and walked back to his house with a wry smile, shaking his head.

Heisenberg

Heisenberg had a notion that you could not be precise about both the location and velocity of a particle at the same time. That's true of people too. I find people, perhaps because we are made up of many particles, are incredibly more complex. It's just tough to pin them down. This is particularly observable in Cosmo. There are moments when I'm fishing when I feel like I have stopped moving. Velocity 0. My location is precise, and everything is moving toward me. There is no here or there, no before and after. Just a moment. I suppose if that happened to a particle, it would be considered inert. But to a Buddhist, that might be enlightenment. I don't know enough about physics or Buddhism to say.

But I do know a few things about my friend Cosmo, and that is enough to say about the complexity of the human soul. I've known Cos since grade school, though we did not really associate much until high school. Cosmo's dad owned a plumbing supply business that included a large warehouse that was a bunch of racks and shelves, that held blue and gray bins of various sizes, that were loaded with pipes, fasteners, joints, valves—you name it. We used the warehouse to congregate and consume our underage six-packs before heading out to whatever event was dominant on the high school social calendar. As often as not, that event involved some sport; and as Cosmo participated in several of them, notably football and basketball, he was occasionally absent for the pre-activities but was normally able to join us for any post-activities.

Cosmo was popular not only for having the keys to the warehouse but also as an athlete and as someone who was attractive to the girls. I guess it was mostly because he had a certain level of confidence and had a certain way of entertaining us with his stories that most just enjoyed being in his company. In his senior year, he started dating one girl in particular, Jean, and it got serious as Jean ended up pregnant. Well, Cosmo's dad was pretty upset with him over that and decided to show it by giving him little support. The upshot of it being that when Cosmo graduated, he enlisted in the Army, married Jean, and left for basic training two days after graduation.

After basic, Cosmo returned home, orders in hand, just in time to see his son born and was sent over to Korea for his first duty. By then, Korea was just a police action, but the action in Vietnam was heavy. That was his second, third, and fourth tours. After four years, Cosmo had made it to sergeant and was done. By then, Cosmo's dad had come to accept the situation for what it was. It was hard to resist his grandson, Jean was a kind and gentle person, and I think Cosmo's dad feared for Cosmo. Anyhow, he found it in his capacity to offer Cosmo a job in the business. Well, sort of. Cosmo's dad got one of the plumbers who bought supplies from him to agree to take Cosmo on as a sort of laborer/apprentice and teach him the trade.

Cosmo took to the trade; within a few years, he started his own business. I still remember the white Ford van with Pipe King painted on the side panels. Sadly, things took a turn for the bad; Jean had ovarian cancer that ultimately took her. It might have been the loss of Jean that softened the heart of Cosmo's dad a bit more because it was about six months after that that Cosmo was offered a share of the plumbing supply business. He signed on, never reciprocating his dad's disdain in him, but at the same time, kept the smaller local plumbing business going. Popular as ever with his outgoing personality, he had established a fairly good business by then, though he did cut back taking care mostly of established residential customers.

Cosmo also gave quite generously to the community. As a veteran, he was deeply committed to veterans who did not fare as well as him. The nearest VA hospital was in the city about forty miles to the east; and Cos, on a regular basis, would load his van with guys who needed therapy, rehabilitation, dialysis, or other outpatient treatments. One thing we did not learn about Cos until much later was that while the guys were undergoing their treatments, Cosmo would go over to the children's hospital where he volunteered as a baby holder. He'd just go and spend a couple of hours holding babies while his comrades in arms received treatment. Maybe he was making up for the time he lost with his own son. The other thing he would do was spend as much time as time would permit at the county home. The old guys just enjoyed getting the local news told with Cosmo's own storytelling skill.

By that time, Cosmo's son, Matt, was around twelve years old or so and was showing signs of following his dad in terms of his athleticism. By the time he entered high school, his athletic ability was well established, eventually earning him a full-ride scholarship to play football at a division 1 college. It was the summer between Matt's junior and senior years at school that the following events occurred.

It was late May when Julie checked in. She was to be a boarder, staying for the summer; she had a summer session teaching job at the college. Julie had a PhD in something or other; I can't say for sure, which again speaks to the complexity of people. It simply wasn't significant or salient to me. Whereas, for her, I reckon it was something important. No doubt she had committed considerable time and effort to accomplishing the credential and it was, in fact, her means to a living. But what I remember best about her was that she was a bright, energetic, and engaging person. She wore a perpetual smile, and while not overbearing, she found it easy to join a conversation on about anything. She was also an attractive woman in particular aspects but not lacking in any, a bit slenderer than my wife, who is the standard by which all women are measured. She had more of a wholesome look than that of a stunning beauty, but one you could not pass without taking notice.

And that is exactly what happened that evening when Cosmo arrived to join Tad, Walt, and me for a drink at the bar. Julie was sitting in the front room, reading something, and she looked up as Cos entered the house and the screen door sprung shut behind him to announce his arrival. She merely looked up and flexed her perpetual smile in his direction as a greeting. His response was a bit more emphatic, and we teased him about it later. He was a bit flustered and befuddled, and we had some laughs, as Cos was usually a suave character. The truth is, he not only noticed Julie but was also stunned and smitten, though we only learned this later. We asked her if she cared to join us, but she declined, as she was going to walk over to the college and get the lay of the land in town.

Well, from that day forward, Cosmo stopped by the house every day, some days twice; it went back to quotidian once he got a bearing on Julie's schedule. Eventually, she did join us on some evenings for a drink. She didn't seem to care much for brown whiskey but had acquired a few bottles of wine, some local beers, and some gin for her summer favorite of gin and tonic, all of which she kept in the bar. After about two to three weeks, it became clear that Cos had difficulty focusing his attention on anything else but her when she was in the room. While she did not display the same attraction to him, she did not seem uncomfortable with Cosmo's attention and did nothing to discourage it.

In fact, as my wife took note of this developing relationship, I sensed she felt more discomfort than Julie. One night, I asked her what was troubling her. As she was explaining, it became clear that there were certain things about Cosmo to which I was blind. Cos never remarried, though at this time he was still south of forty years old. Rumor had it that most of Cos's plumbing customers were single, though some were married, middle-aged women. Apparently, these particular women had some serious plumbing problems. According to the rumors, the moniker Pipe King had less to do with the plumbing business than it did with a certain part of Cosmo's anatomy. The wife referred to him as an "ass-bandit." I felt like someone on the outside looking in but began to see the rumors as more of rounding out the story rather than conflicting with my limited reading. I liked Cos and I guess preferred to stay on the outside looking in; my wife shared this view but had become somewhat protective of Julie as we had got to know and like her.

The summer rolled on, and Cos and Julie were in status quo, though by now, everyone was tuned in to the game of cat and mouse that we all agreed was going on. Time was running out though, as Julie would be leaving toward the end of August. While Cos and Julie might not have felt it, the rest of us, as observers, were feeling an increased pressure. In addition to any velocity these two particles had, we had our own that clearly influenced our observations. Heisenberg may have had the uncertainty thing right about location and velocity, but kudos to Einstein for his views on relativity and the need to consider the location and velocity of the observer.

One morning, after having walked Timmy, I walked into the kitchen to take my second cup of coffee. I found my wife sitting at the kitchen table with red puffy eyes. She had clearly been crying, so I poured a cup and sat down beside her. I didn't have to ask before she broke like a dam. It all came tumbling out.

"Cos is dying!"

"What! How do you know that?"

"Julie told me!"

"Julie, how does she know?"

"He told her. He's got cancer!"

Now I had a tough time believing that Cosmo would reveal something like that without telling us, his close friends, first.

"Back up. Why did Julie tell you this?"

I was only a little less surprised that someone would reveal something like this that was obviously shared in trust. Then my wife proceeded to explain.

A while after I left that morning with Timmy, my wife heard the screen door slam shut. She waited a bit, anticipating me or someone to walk in, but failing that, she walked to the front door. And all she saw was Cosmo, about a half block away crossing the street. This struck her as odd, but she had quite a bit of velocity on a particular trajectory that led her right to Julie.

Well, it turned out that Julie and Cos finally succumbed to the pressure we were all feeling. Cosmo and Julie lingered at the bar after the rest of us said our good nights. We thought Cos had left and gone home, and while we were ultimately right about his location, we were wrong about the velocity. He ended up staying that night with Julie. Now I won't say our boarders never had guests, but we kind of discouraged it, and someone like Cosmo certainly would have been aware of our view on such visitations. As my wife started to clarify this view to Julie, Julie stopped her and started to explain.

Julie never intended to get involved with Cosmo. Yes, he was nice; she took his interest sincerely and was flattered by it. It wasn't that she was not attracted either, but she knew she would be leaving and likely never see him again. It wasn't in her nature to become intimate knowing this was the future. However, she was overwhelmed when Cos, in what was his final thrust to her parries, asked her to "Humor an old man dying of cancer."

With that knowledge, she not only would likely never see him again but also felt the need to reciprocate the extent of his feeling, knowing the attention and time he doted on her as he was facing his limited future. For whatever reason, he made her such a priority; she wanted to answer in some measure that came close. Julie had expressed no remorse in her choice but found the situation too sad to endure. She had decided that she would leave the next day. Her course at the college was done, so she spent the rest of the day saying goodbye to friends and colleagues and took her leave the following morning.

We were still reeling from the news when Cos arrived the next day at his usual time, unaware that Julie had left. He looked a bit sheepish when I mentioned her departure and invited him to join me for a drink. I could see his increasing discomfort as I struggled to find an on-ramp to my destination, so out of sympathy and a complete lack of tact, I let it out. "Cos, why didn't you tell us you were dying of cancer?"

He stood up; his eyes popped open. "What!"

"Julie told us you asked her"—and I quoted—"to humor an old man dying of cancer."

An awkward silence followed, and then he broke it, saying, "I'm not old."

"And not dying of cancer?"

"No."

"Then why did you tell that sweet woman such a lie?"

"It's not a lie."

"Cos! Then what kind of bullshit is this?"

"Well, you know I visit the county home at least once a week. There are plenty of old men dying of cancer who will be humored by this story."

"Out! Out! Out!"

Those were the last words I spoke to Cosmo for about a month. I could never come clean with my wife; she asked me about Cosmo, and in my heart, I almost hoped he would contract cancer. I felt so poorly of him. Again, got the location right even if we were off a bit on velocity. Anyhow, I needed some plumbing done, which I was going to try myself but found I needed some supplies that I could either buy from Cosmo's store or in another store forty miles away. Being angry is one thing, but I try not to have it result in self-inflicted harm. So I went to the store, half hoping that Cosmo wouldn't be there, but he was.

Turned out that Julie's next teaching gig was at the college Matt was attending. Cos never missed a game, and as velocities and locations would have it, they collided. Julie, of course, knew Matt was on the team, so I am not sure that she had not set a vector to alter the odds of this happening. Cos did not explain to me what had happened; either he told the truth, had a miraculous recovery, or somewhere in between. But he and Julie apparently reconciled their views and feelings, and I guess that is all right for me.

Fishing with Jim and Larry

I don't travel much anymore. I guess I live vicariously through the travels of those who come to us at the parsonage to scratch that itch. And it costs less to do it that way. Some of those have made travels I could only hope to make, and some I hope never to make. But one thing can make me enthusiastic about travel or at least muster the energy it takes to get headed in a certain direction; that is fishing.

Jim is an old friend who never lacked the energy to get headed in the right direction for fishing either. Though one time, he did doubt me. He, Larry, and I were going to head out one morning, and the night before, we agreed we would get an early start. I told Jim I would pick him up at his mailbox at 4:30 a.m. At the time, I lived in Pennsylvania, across the street and two houses down from Jim. Now the rest of this I only learned later. About a half hour before the appointed time, Jim rolled out of bed. As he was making his way to the head, he peered out of his window. A glance in the direction of my house gave no testimony to my being active. No doubts yet, but the seed was planted. In the quiet of the morning, when the only sounds to distract you are the toilet flush, the shower hiss, and your razor scraping whiskers from your face, the mind has unused capacity. Capacity to speculate. By the time Jim had finished his shit, shower, and shave, another glance at my house, with still no proof of life, was confirmation of the fully blossomed speculation, which by now had ripened to a certitude, that this whole "mailbox at four thirty" was just a ruse. I'm sure he had visions of me rolling over in my warm bed, chuckling at him standing at his mailbox. "Who fishes at four thirty anyhow?" he was asking himself.

At 4:28, when I flipped on the light outside my front door to guide me to my truck, I opened the door to my house and saw Jim standing behind the glass of the storm door at the entrance to his home. I threw my gear into the truck, started the engine, backed out of my driveway, and drove about fifty yards to Jim's mailbox. Jim got in, grunted his good morning, and proceeded to sit there. At the time, I let it pass as Jim not being a morning person. I learned later that he was pissed off, at first at me, but that had dissipated by the time he was in the truck and had been projected onto himself for getting so worked up.

I learned all this years later when my dad had died. Dad had died in February, and unfortunately, the ground was too frozen to dig his grave. So in April, I had to return for the interment. Jim offered to join me for the seven-hour drive, suggesting we could do a little fishing along the way. "Maybe the steelhead and salmon will still be running out of the lake," he said. As it turned out, the snowmelt had the rivers and streams running so high and fast there was no fishing to be done. He told me the story about the four thirty rendezvous on that trip. It was nice to have Jim along for the ride—to fill the silence and to dilute my sorrow with some laughter.

Anyhow, after I picked up Jim, we went on to Larry's, had some breakfast, and got on to our fishing for the day. Larry was my first, and lasting, friend when I moved to Pennsylvania. I took a position with a company in Philadelphia after spending four years in Europe scratching an entrepreneurial itch and learning some of the French language in the process. I had no connection to Philly, but there was a good opportunity there. I was living temporarily in an apartment in the city and walked to the office my first day. First days everywhere, I would guess, are about the same. They welcomed me, gave me a pile of paperwork for the various employee benefits to fill out, and showed me to my office. In my first job, I worked with about sixty-five colleagues; when I went to Europe, I worked with about fifteen; in Philadelphia, I had about four hundred new friends to make. It's easy when you are one of sixty-five or fifteen to meet people; others notice you. With four hundred, it's easy to be ignored, let someone else do it.

Well, on that day, Larry did it. As the lunch hour approached, I began to think about heading out for something to eat. Then it occurred to me, my office was so deep in the labyrinth I was not even sure if I could find my way back to the reception area. I was about to call the receptionist to ask for directions. Fortunately for me, Larry was accomplished at urban orienteering and somehow found his way to my office. He announced himself by saying, "I heard there was a new guy joining us. Want to go to lunch?" First and lasting.

This is why on an October morning, I loaded my gear into the truck, whistled for Timmy, then yelled for Timmy, and finally grabbed him by the collar and dragged his ass to the truck, and headed off to Pennsylvania to go fishing with Jim and Larry. It's about a seven-hour drive to Southeastern, Pennsylvania, from home, but what a beautiful drive it is at this time of the year. The air is cooler and has a rich scent of the decaying foliage, and while the days are trending shorter, they seem brighter by the contrast of autumn's colors everywhere present. I arrived midafternoon at Larry's house, in time for a little nap before Larry returned from work. Jim, Larry, and I met for a beer and some dinner and laid out our plans for tomorrow.

First, we agreed we would pick up Jim at his mailbox around four thirty; that set off about an hour of stories that never fail to improve with each telling and brought us around to one of our favorite haunts, Valley Creek in Valley Forge Park. It was thus decided we would fish there in the morning. Valley Creek became one of our favorites because of its proximity to home and work. That is, we could easily stop or meet there after work as we headed home. The stream itself is not a large one but has an interesting history. More than 250 years ago, the lower end of Valley Creek sustained Washington's Continental Army. Certain stretches of the creek are within a few feet of Lafayette's headquarters during the Revolutionary War. That's the good part of the history and demonstrates how nature sustains us in the most desperate of times. In more recent times, it has been polluted with cyanide and, most recently, when PCBs were spilled into the stream by Conrail. Because of its limestone bed, Valley Creek has been able to recover from these abuses. Today, stream-bred brown trout, wild but not native fish, thrive in the stream.[1]

The next morning, we picked up Jim around nine and by nine forty-five were streamside assembling our rods, tightening on reels, running line and leader through guides, and tying on tippet and flies. I did not see anything hatching on the water, so I tied on a chartreuse woolly bugger—a nice big bright streamer for a nice big, fat brown. An interesting, and I find appealing, aspect of fly-fishing is that it has its communal moments (e.g., driving to and from the stream, assembling and disassembling your gear), and it has its solitary moments, actual fishing itself. So we headed off in diverse directions to find our own pool to fish or riffle to wade.

Jim and Larry had it a bit more solitary than I did because I had Timmy along. It's not customary to fish with a dog, but truth be told, despite my efforts at training, Timmy was about as useful fishing as he was hunting. Just as truthfully, he did no harm. He stayed out of the water except to take a drink now and then, and he was usually busy busting through brush several feet away from the stream bank. I could usually hear him, and because of the training that stuck, he would check back with me every so often just to keep me in sight.

I was walking upstream, along the edge of the stream, fishing some shallow, slow-running riffles. I was casting from one bank to the other, stripping the streamer across the riffles. I had what I thought might be a few hits, but it could have just as easily been a leaf or twig being pushed along in the water. Up ahead, I saw a bend in the stream; and where it turned, there was a deep undercut of a large sycamore. The water was flowing off a riffle into a quiet pool, and it was lapping gently against the exposed black roots of the sycamore.

My eyes had to adjust from the nervous energy of the riffles to the calm rhythm of the pool. As they did, I could see among the undulations an occasional rise of a big brown trout. He was coming up to something; a more discerning look showed me some small midges dancing above the water, some of which were lying upon the

---

[1]   Acknowledgment to Charles R. Meck—*Pennsylvania Trout Streams and Their Hatches*, Second Edition—for the historical information.

surface. I still had my gaudy woolly bugger tied on and was too lazy to switch, so I cast it into the riffles flowing into the pool and let it drift in by the force of the water. Nothing. I slowly stripped it out and cast again. Same result. Try again, definition of insanity, except in fly-fishing.

Again, I began to strip in the fly. *Bang*, fish on. I pulled up on the rod tip to set the hook, and that big hog responded by pulling back and dropping to the bottom of the pool. Judging by the amount of line he pulled off with him, I put the pool at eight to ten feet deep. He didn't have anywhere to go, as the pool was bound both upstream and downstream by some shallow riffles, at least too shallow for a fish of his size to navigate under duress. So he swam frantically at the bottom of the pool, and I fought just to keep some steady pressure on him and to hasten his tiring. Finally, he did, and I was able to bring him to the surface. While I removed the hook, I took the time to appreciate him and then released him back into the pool.

As I watched him descend into the dark of the pool, my sensory circle began to expand. While the sights, sounds, and scents of my surroundings enlarged, it occurred to me something was missing. I could no longer hear Timmy. I whistled for him, called out—nothing. I tried again—insanity. I walked a few steps, continuing upstream. About thirty feet up from the sycamore pool, I saw a small trail, a bit bigger than a deer trail and made much more distinct by what looked like something had been dragged along it. The stone and dirt were scraped in one direction and streaked with blood. At first, I thought maybe a hunter might have taken a deer near here and had dragged it out. I wasn't too sure of this, as I thought it early for bow season, but then I speculated that it being a national park, maybe they had a special regulated hunt this time of year. Then it occurred to me that Timmy might have picked up this scent, narrowed his focus like I had on the fish, and had followed the trail. Off I went to retrieve my dog.

Since this was unfamiliar territory for me, I thought it might be wise to set some bearings. You can use an analog watch as a crude compass by pointing the hour hand directly at the sun. You then take a line that is halfway between the hour hand and the twelve o'clock position, and that line is your north/south orientation. Since I was in the northern hemisphere, putting the equator to the south of me, I put the sun at my back, standing along my north/south line, and got oriented. This put the stream southwest of me. The blood-streaked trail was heading north-northeast, so off I went. I counted sixty-two paces in this general direction as the trail led through woods transitioning to shrub and, eventually, tallgrass meadow as I moved away from the stream and came to what looked like an unimproved road. Well, more like well-worn tire tracks with a grass median kept short by the undercarriage of passing vehicles. It was here the blood trail ended, and the road veered off in a due-north direction to my left. I quickly confirmed my sense of bearing with my watch.

I was gaining confidence in my theory regarding a hunter and quarry, figuring this was where the deer was loaded onto a car or truck. Then to the north, I heard a voice, a car door slam shut, and the crunch of gravel as the car moved away. Feeling confident too that I could find my way back to this point, I headed north along the road, thinking maybe I would run into someone who might have seen Timmy. I continued to count paces, and at eighty-seven, the road took a left at about ninety degrees, putting me on a due-west bearing. Ahead I saw the upper branches of a lone oak tree above the tassels on the tallgrass and made mental note of it as a prominent landmark as I headed down the road toward it.

As I continued down the road, I noticed that away from the low-lying creek and out of the cover of the wooded buffer, the wind was blowing pretty good. The grass was bending in the wind as if to listen to a distant voice, and it replied with a muted rustling voice of the wind against its tassels. More and more of the tree revealed itself, uncovered by the grass as I got nearer. As I was looking directly at the tree, a swift wind swirled and parted the grass; and in a flashing but distinct moment, I saw it. Like when lightning on a dark night illuminates everything for an instant, a body was hanging in the tree. Just as fast, it was gone as the grass closed to conceal this grizzly ornament.

A shot of adrenaline coursed through my body; I could feel my pulse quicken and sensed throbbing blood in my temples. My mouth went dry, and I crouched to the ground in a defensive stance. From one moment to the next, I gained control of my heart and breathing too, the rational functions of my brain. I told myself that this was not real and I misapprehended. I would check it out. Because I had not fully convinced myself, I moved stealthily into the grass. It was certainly tall enough, and the wind aided me by concealing whatever movement or sound I made as I worked closer to the tree. I noticed that in the grass, I could hear better too. It sounded like there was someone in the grass moving closer to me. I could not tell from what direction the movement was coming, but I was gaining on the tree. Finally, I was about three feet from a small clearing around the tree and could see through the grass to the base of the tree. Next to the tree was a bench, the kind you would find at a softball field; on the bench were two unused nooses with a long coil of rope on the ground. Whatever it was I saw hanging from the tree was still there but concealed by the trunk.

I moved slowly to my right and, to my horror, saw what appeared to be hands, bound, behind the back of a person. I shifted again to my right, and the body of a person clad in black, and hooded, with a noose around its neck came into view, twisting in the wind. Then in an instant, I heard something rushing toward me in the grass. I leaped up from my crouch, turned my back to the tree, and ran as fast as I could. Again, the adrenaline was fueling my movement and entire physiology. I crossed over the road and, for an instant, considered turning right and letting it guide me back to the trail. But I could still hear my pursuer crashing through the grass behind me, so I opted for the grass ahead of me and disappeared into its cover.

I kept running and, before long, came to another opening. I did not think this was good as I would be exposed and headed toward the nearest access to the tallgrass. But this was more than a clearing. As I ran through it, I saw a freshly dug, shallow, open grave with a body thrown in it with the limbs of its left side and cocked head not fully interred. I did not stop to study this, as I could hear my pursuer in chase and not relenting. Up ahead, I could see treetops and ran toward them. I had made it back to the wooded buffer of the stream but had no idea where in relation to my egress. So much for my measured paces and the watch as compass. Worse still, I could still hear someone coming through the grass. I found some fallen timber, climbed over it, rolled under it, and hoped it would conceal me.

I heard the footsteps slow and tread more deliberately. I assumed they had made it out of the grass and, now encumbered by both the standing and fallen timber, had to maneuver around it. I could not see, but I could hear, and the steps were getting nearer. It sounded as there might be two of them. I held my breath and could now hear them breathing—panting? Next thing I felt was something cold pressing against my neck and a rough tongue licking the sweat that was pouring down it. Timmy. Timmy was my pursuer. While this gave brief relief, I was still trying to process the macabre scene I had wandered into and flew from. I had to find Jim and Larry and call the police. I gathered myself and made my way back to the stream by venturing further into the woods, taking the downslope of the land. I did not immediately recognize the place at which I arrived but surmised I should follow the water downstream. In time, I came to the bloody trail and, just beyond it, the sycamore pool.

From this point, I quickly made it back to the car we had traveled in. I had a phone that was left in Larry's car; and he, of course, had locked it. With my mind racing and nowhere to go, the imagination filled in a lot of the blanks that were left with my hasty observations and flight. I don't know how long it was, but Jim was the first to return. I played back for him my entire experience, adding gruesome details here and leaving out unimportant ones there, like how I ran my ass off eluding Timmy. Finally, Larry returned. I started to tell my story again as he fished inside his waders to find his keys to unlock his door so that I could call the police.

At first, Larry had a tough time following my very animated, agitated telling; but eventually, he grabbed a thread and showed a look of comprehension but surprised me and Jim by laughing like a damn fool. For an instant, I had this weird thought that Larry might have been the killer, and this was the part of the movie where he offed me and Jim. There were two empty nooses at the tree. When he stopped laughing, he said nothing to explain his behavior but suggested instead of calling the police we drive to the park ranger's office. Jim thought this made sense, and besides, I could not get a signal on my phone, so reluctantly I got into the back seat of the car. Larry drove out to the main park road and then turned right off the road to an old covered bridge that crossed the stream. The bridge was a one-lane covered bridge, so we had to stop to make sure no one was coming the other way. Once over the bridge, we took another right turn, down a dirt road; now that weird feeling was coming back. That was until we came to a parking lot, at the entrance of which was a sign:

MontCo Junior Achievement
HAUNTED HAYRIDES
October 24–31
8:00 p.m.–Midnight[2]

So with Jim and Larry laughing at me and me appreciating that a dog is indeed a man's best friend, we headed off to the local brewhouse to plan the next day's fishing.

Day 2

This time, we really did start out at four thirty because we were fishing Pine Creek. We chose Pine Creek because of its unusually good fishing that includes brown, rainbow, and brook trout. And because it would get me a little more than half the way home, while Jim and Larry would have to do some backtracking at the end of the day. So I followed Jim and Larry out, with Timmy in my truck to keep me company.

We were on the water by eight thirty. One of the nice things about Pine Creek is that it has many tributary streams. These trib streams—while smaller than Pine Creek, which can run anywhere from fifty to one hundred feet wide—can be filthy with fish. The fish may not get as big, but they are plentiful, and I've found you are

---

[2]   Acknowledgment to Robin Wall Kimmerer—*Braiding Sweetgrass*, from which this story was adapted and appropriated.

more likely to hook up with some brookies on these little streams. Moreover, many of the tribs are limestone, which means healthier water with more abundant hatches even this late in the year. I started off on the Pine but diverted onto one of these tribs about a half mile upstream from where we stepped in. No need for a compass or bearings; I figured today I would just stay on the water.

A wonderful thing happens when you step into a stream. Naturally, you have to move a little bit slower just to navigate the slippery cobble beneath your feet and the force of the water against your legs. But the world slows down too, things get closer, and you become more connected. You feel the force of the water pushing against you. You hear the wind moving through the trees, knocking the leaves from the trees, falling like huge colorful snowflakes. You even become conscious of your own breathing and heartbeat mixed in with the squirrels rustling in the leaves and the songs of the birds.

I was not disappointed with the decision to go on the tributary. While the water was low and the flow gentle, I did find some nice little pools that were holding beautiful brook trout that were interested in all that I threw at them at the end of my fly line. I was able to fish dry flies most of the morning, casting upstream and letting them drift back toward me. Watching the flies moved along by an almost-invisible current into a pool then go into a swirl in an eddy before coming to a complete stop. Long enough for a brook trout to rise slowly and sip it in. There was no strike; I had to see it, set the hook by gently and quickly lift the tip of the rod, and then let the fish tire out as it swam laps in the confines of the pool.

The problem with fishing in pools is that after a couple of hook-ups and the commotion that follows, just about all the other fish catch on that something is up. They get wary and head to the bottom of the pool, no longer seduced by the fly you are drifting over their heads. So you move on. I passed a good couple of hours doing just that. I was continuing upstream without really noticing that I had gone from a nice broad wooded buffer on both sides of the stream to sheer walls that rose, it seemed, to almost one hundred feet or more. I found myself in a canyon of sorts. The other thing I noticed is that Timmy was nowhere in sight. He usually would be tearing through the woods and brush on or near the stream bank, but I must have lost him when I moved into the canyon.

In high water, I prefer to stay out of canyons, as you can get caught in a flash flood; and with stone walls to channel the water and no banks to mitigate the surge and force, you can get swept away easily. But as I said, the water was low, so I decided to continue. My thinking was that this water not being easily accessible, there might be some good fishing on some native brookies. Up ahead, I saw a pool in which to test that theory. As I came up to the pool, I started to cast, about sixty feet to where the water entered the pool. It took some good double hauls to get that much line out with a light dry fly on, but I had a nice straight canyon-lined corridor behind me—no wind to fight or trees or shrubs to catch my line. What trees there were, were on top of the canyon, providing a canopy from the sun, which was further darkened by the stratified stone walls that lined the stream on both sides.

Almost immediately, a fish took my fly, and the usual dance was on. Just keep the tip up, a little tension, and she will begin to follow my lead. I noticed then that to one side of the stream, there were some trees lying in the water. They looked like hemlocks that had either fallen from the top of the cliffs or had been washed downstream in a storm. It wasn't clear what they were snagged on, but my fish was heading under them, and I feared I would lose her, being that I had some light leader and tippet tied on. To my surprise, that fish went under the logs and kept running. She started to run off thirty to forty feet of line. Finally, she did break off and was gone.

With the excitement of the fish gone, I could again hear my heart beating and the breath my lungs were pushing in and out, but little else. There was no wind in the canyon, no trees or leaves to be rustled by wind or squirrel, no song of birds—just a gentle lap of water against the dark canyon walls. The entire universe got smaller and closer, and I felt as if I had been swallowed. Then it occurred to me that for the amount of line that fish ran off, that must be one of the deepest pools in all of Pennsylvania. I waded a bit closer, but the water was staying steady just below my knees. When I got about ten feet from the trees, I began to see light shining through from behind and beneath them. I could make out the outline of an arch in the stone behind the trees that was veiled in the grass and other of nature's detritus that had got hung up in the hemlock branches. In fact, the trees had become snagged in the arch.

I walked a bit further upstream and pushed on one of the trees that once moved into the current and quickly slid away from the cliff wall, pulling the other tree with it, to reveal an arch, a gateway into the cliff that was about two to three feet above the water. Bending down, I could see a pool of water extending a little distance, a bit of a bank to the water and plenty of daylight. This was not a cave; on the other side, it opened onto something, but I could see too little to tell what. That fish had not run deep; she ran long into that opening.

As did I—cautiously though. I still wasn't sure how deep the pool ran. And while the water rose from my knees to my waist, I only had to crouch a little to get under the archway. I suspect at normal water levels this arch is not much exposed, if at all. If only moments before I had been swallowed by the earth or laid in its dark womb, I had just now been born into the most beautiful place in all the universe. I waded into a pond, surrounded by cattails. As the pond floor transitioned from the cobble of the creek to the mud of the marsh, I emerged from the cattails that were anchored there. I stood at the edge of a meadow that opened before me. It was bathed in sun. As I looked around, I saw fall goldenrod; blue, rose, and violet asters; and purple ironweed as if in an impressionist painting. The walls of the canyon that lined the creek were still there, behind a veil of shrubs and trees, spreading into a bowl a thousand feet in diameter, framing this hidden, verdant, and fecund crater.

I lay down in the meadow, looked up, and watched the clouds drift slowly by. Again, the birds were singing, their sound falling on silence, sound on silence, not interrupting but a continuity of sound and silence. Time passed into the moment, from the past into the future, with the only presence being the moment. I could smell the wildflowers and the moist earth upon which I lay. I turned to look at the earth, and the world became smaller and industrious. The roots of the grasses and plants penetrating the earth, searching for nourishment; ants, grasshoppers, and a variety of insects moving about with purpose, though I knew not what it might be. I turned back to the clouds, heard the screech of a hawk, and the world became larger, as I shrunk imagining how I would look to an eye from the sky. If I could be seen at all. I tried to look beyond the sky and could see nothing at all.

I wondered if I could become as nothing at all. What if I just stayed here—passed like time into a singular moment, sound on silence, a cloud passing in the sky? Cattails were an excellent food source. There were fish in the pond; and no doubt, deer, rabbit, or squirrel found their way in here. With a snare and my knife, I would have meat; and if I foraged, I suppose I might find some walnut or hickory trees to provide nuts. Here, I imagined, I could subsist on nothing but by my effort and what the earth gave me. Then I heard Timmy barking. I must have fallen asleep; a little woods nap never hurt anyone. But when I looked up, the clouds had turned to streaky wisps and were pink like the color of cotton candy. My eyes were finally drawn to Timmy's bark; he stood at the top of one of the cliffs, some one hundred feet or more above me, yelping.

I got up, and once I started moving, he stopped barking. I kept looking back at him, and he back at me, as I moved to the pond and the arch that led me back to the creek. There was no way for Timmy to come down the sheer walls that formed the crater or to descend to the creek. He followed me from atop the ridge as I began my downstream walk. As I was not stopping to fish, I made it back to the cars relatively fast. I would guess it took thirty to thirty-five minutes to get to the cars; Jim and Larry were waiting. I guess I must have taken a little nap, as it was getting on near six thirty. They were a bit pressed for time, owing to the four-hour return trip; I had only about three hours to make. We said our goodbyes and committed to doing it again.

As I drove back, with only Timmy to keep me company, again silence created a void for thought. I was still trying to process my experience. I was at such peace when I returned to the cars but could, or chose to, say nothing. The exigency of time kept me from trying to relate my experience to Jim and Larry, but honestly, even with all the time in the world, I don't know if I could have found or organized the words. I'm still not sure that I can.

I thought about the peace I felt as I considered becoming nothing—living off what the earth would provide and by my own effort. I realized this is not nothing though. It is a relationship with the earth that I do not, at present, actively develop. I have other relationships—husband, father, friend—that I have developed, and some with considerable effort. But it made me realize I still have this relationship with the earth. I breathe the air, drink the water, and the source of all my nourishment is from it. In fact, the produce of nature costs nothing; it costs no one anything. Granted it would take my effort or, in fact, someone else's effort to render most of nature's produce to a useable product for my consumption. I know both Adam Smith and Karl Marx covered this territory. This was not the epiphany to me. What was is that I do have a relationship with the earth. Maybe I just hadn't thought enough about it.

So it got me thinking about the relationships I had: husband to wife, father to child, friend to friend. Connected, as sound to silence, day to night, spring to summer, sun to rain—each partaking in the other and shaped by it.[3] The relationships of which I was most conscious were driven by a choice, the volitional force of love. The others I was beginning to think of were driven by an equally mysterious force of nature. But what of my relationship with the earth? Certainly, nature has bound us, and I partake amply of what the earth has given. How has the earth partaken of what I have to give? How have I shaped the earth? I am still working on the answer to these questions. I have realized, however, I will have to exercise the volitional force of love in this relationship to balance the exchange.

When I love, I do not consume to the exhaustion of the other; I nourish and nurture the other, if only to keep them healthy and with me. I surrender some of myself to the other so that together we are greater than alone. As light surrenders to dark to make the day, as spring surrenders to summer and summer to autumn, autumn to winter and back to spring, a cycle turns; tell me where it begins or

---

[3]   Acknowledgment to Wallace Stevens, "It Must Change, IV."

ends. From rain and sun arise the meadow and magnificent trees. I guess I will start by being a little gentler with the earth and examine my acts as acts of love. Can't go wrong with that.

Forrest Gump

In the early 1990s, there was a movie about a character who, by circumstance, shows up in some epic situations; but what made the story interesting was that the story was about him and the epic situations were in the background. Moviegoers could relate because they too had lives that were going on while these epic events were occurring. Over the years, we have had some guests that were Forrest Gumps of sorts. That is, based on their telling anyway, their ordinary lives had juxtaposed them in some unusual events. I don't know how true any of these stories are, though they are credible and certainly worthy of retelling. There are three that stand out, and I have even given them titles.

The Jesus Gene. Now this one comes from a businessman, Tom Doyle, who was visiting a professor at the college. If I recall correctly, he was here to evaluate whether his company was interested in investing in some research project in which this professor was engaged. I came to understand that this was Tom's job, to find academic research that might have commercial applications. If the research proved promising in his view, they would provide research funding in exchange for a license to develop commercial applications. By way of explaining what this meant, he provided an example from several years back.

In the 1970s, there was some research done on the Shroud of Turin. It is held by some that this shroud was the very one that the crucified Jesus Christ was wrapped in for his entombment. After his resurrection, this shroud was found in his tomb; the stains upon it bore what to the modern eye looked like a photographic negative image of Christ. Obviously, this would be a very holy relic of the church; and likewise, it drew the attention of many skeptics. Initially, the object of the research was to use scientific methods to demonstrate its authenticity, for example, using carbon dating and analysis of the materials to ascertain its age.

Now this research had been completed, but what wasn't part of the published result was that the researchers had collected genetic material from the shroud. The researchers, being curious by nature, wanted to continue testing this genetic material to see what they could learn from it. No one, at least initially, thought that they could prove this material was of Christ, nor were they confident in what it would reveal of the person to whom it belonged. It was so old, decayed, etc. to be sure of its quality without more testing. But imagine if it was Christ's and they could tell us of his phenotypes (e.g., eye and hair color) and whether he had certain diseases or ailments and more. This proposition excited the interest of a certain medical forensics company, and Tom was sent to investigate.

It happened that the technologies being developed by the company could be significantly advanced by this research, and simultaneously, they would add great efficiency to the work of the scientific team, not to mention the marketing impact of Christ's halo. The project had to be moved to India for several reasons. Chief among them was that was where the company had invested to do genetic research, largely because of government regulation and ethical concerns in the United States. There was a hidden agenda as well.

This company had access to a vast, unconnected catalogue of genetic materials. This catalogue included other samples drawn from relics of the church over time in testing like what had been performed on the Shroud of Turin. The reliquary included, among other things, Veronica's veil, thorns from Christ's crown, and more. What the material from the shroud could provide was corroboration of the claim that this and the other genetic material were indeed of Christ, or at least the same person, and, potentially, missing sequences so that a full DNA strand could be completed. And indeed, it was.

With this, the goals of the project had been vastly exceeded. The company was able to claim a technology that could analyze, recombine, and prove the veracity of a sample and, what's more, tell a story about Christ that has never been told. A small group of company scientists were, however, not satisfied to stop there. They used the DNA developed, now a complete strand, to clone Jesus. The fertilized in vitro egg was implanted into a woman. This woman, in a crisis of faith, fled before the child was born.

For years, a search went on for the woman and the child, with no success. Tom had long since lost the thread on this story, and no one who might be knowledgeable was saying what they knew, so he had hit a dead end and stopped his pursuit. He only supposed that besides making belief in a virgin birth more credible, it just took science to do what God could do two thousand years ago; if this were the Second Coming of Christ, he would reveal himself in his own time. I look forward to that.

Palace Intrigue. A few years back, the summer of '81, maybe '82, we had a couple who was traveling through. They had spent the day up at Niagara Falls and were heading the next day to the Pro Football Hall of Fame in Canton, Ohio. They were not Americans, not that it matters. I would guess Middle Eastern of some sort. They were taking in Americana, and it must have been '81 because they wanted to talk about Ronald Reagan being elected president.

I tend not to engage in political discussions, and what with our just having got back our hostages from Iran a few months prior and these folks being, apparently, from the Middle East, I decided it would be best to not engage in this line of discussion. However, they persisted, like a kid with something to say but looking for a way for you to bring it up. They could contain it no longer, and she burst forth that they had seen the Shah of Iran, Mohammad Reza Pahlavi, in Niagara Falls. I politely told them they were wrong; really, what I said was "Gee, I thought he died of cancer about a year ago." It's usually better to confront someone with contradictory facts than just tell them they are wrong. They should be able to figure that out for themselves. But they one-upped me. What they told me next—again, I have no way of ascertaining the truth—seemed at least credible.

They were visiting a memorial that was set up to remember the hostages. As they were walking around, they spotted an older gentleman, and she remarked to him that this man looked a lot like the Shah. Well, it turned out the Shah was someone they knew personally; in fact, the Shah was a second cousin or something like that. They decided to get closer to the man they thought was the Shah to confirm their suspicions, and as they did, it was unmistakable. The Shah betrayed a look of recognition and surprise. The Shah smiled faintly, put on sunglasses, turned, and walked away. Reinforced in their suspicion, they took encouragement and followed him. The Shah went to an isolated area of the park; conceding that he was not going to escape the couple, he stopped and stood at the rail, looking out at the falls. They approached; he removed his sunglasses and, with a look of deep concern, faced them.

The Shah greeted them warmly and, with concern and confidence, relayed the following story. He had, in fact, not died. His whole death was staged. He went on to explain. Operatives within the Reagan campaign had struck a deal with the revolutionaries in Iran to turn over the Shah in exchange for the hostages when and if Reagan was elected. The likelihood that Reagan would be elected was significantly increased if the hostages were held because their captivity made Jimmy Carter, the incumbent running for reelection against Reagan, a captive in respect of waging a campaign. Moreover, the longer the hostages were held, the weaker this made Carter look. The Carter campaign caught wind of this scheme and approached the Shah to propose they stage his death. The endgame of this would be, perhaps, with the Shah out of the picture, the revolutionaries would free the hostages and thereby free Carter. The Shah's death by cancer was announced in June. Whether the Iranians ever came to know the truth of his death became irrelevant, for by now they had gained leverage and were interested in seeing Reagan as the next US president. Accordingly, the hostages were held until the day of Reagan's inauguration.

Ironically, in Reagan's second term, it seems the Iranians were able to use this leverage to address Reagan's own hostage crisis. The Iranians were instrumental in securing the release of seven US hostages in Lebanon. This was done in exchange for weapon sales channeled through Israel to Iran, contrary to an embargo initially imposed by Carter and reaffirmed by Reagan early in his presidency. This was the first leg of the scandal known as Iran-Contra.

The Night Of. Back in the early '70s, there was a young man who played football for the Buffalo Bills, a running back, O. J. Simpson. During the years 1981 to 1999, the Bills used to have their summer training camp at the college in town. In 1996, during one of the summer camps, we had a boarder who was a sportswriter for one of the major newspapers or magazines; I can't remember which. Well, anyhow, one night, as Cos, Walt, and I were enjoying some tasty beverages, Sam—that was the writer's name—came in. Since we were already two pours in, I was feeling particularly convivial, and I offered Sam a dram of Jameson. He accepted. It didn't take long, but soon enough, the discussion turned to O. J. and his acquittal in the prior year for that awful murder of his wife and Ron Goldman. Now we had mixed sentiments and opinions about whether the jury reached the right decision, but Sam was insistent that they did. Initially, we just chalked this up to his being a big sports fan and, in particular, a fan of O. J.'s. But it turned out that there was more to support his convictions that O. J. should not have been convicted.

Yes, Sam had covered the Bills for a long time, including the time that O. J. played. And while he did not have a strong personal relationship with O. J., during those years, he got to know many of the players fairly well. Among them was one of O. J.'s teammates, Al Cowlings, who famously was at the wheel of the white Ford Bronco that America watched drive around Los Angeles, California. Shortly after the acquittal, Sam came across Al, and Al gave to him what I guess you would call the rest of the story.

O. J. was there—that was why the Bruno Magli shoe prints ultimately were damning—but what the Juice could not tell you was who committed the murder. Or, we should say, would not tell you for fear of the safety of his and Nicole's children. You see, Nicole had some known substance abuse problems and, as is often the case, started to have some difficulties with her suppliers. She had become increasingly vocal about these suppliers, and because of her high profile, they felt she needed to be silenced. At first, they tried threats, but she was not turning the volume down. In fact, her behavior escalated. So much so that O. J. became involved and did what he could to shut her up. The night of the murder, he had a brief confrontation with her at a restaurant over the matter. But knowing a public place was not the right place to air this out, he left. However, the supply guys—there were two of them—wanted greater and immediate assurances that she understood the need for silence. So they persuaded O. J. that this issue had to be resolved now and followed him to her house. He called her down to continue their discussion, but by the time she hit the street, she was in a rage.

Things went bad. Goldman, who was in Nicole's apartment, came down; and now things had cascaded into a disaster. Both Nicole and Ron met their demise, and O. J. was there. He was then warned that if he ever spoke of this, his children would meet a similar fate. At that point, O. J. drove to his friend, A. C. Cowlings, and they decided it would be best to disappear. And with A. C. at the wheel, we all know what happened next.

Again, not sure if any of this is true, but the stories have enough to be credible, which makes them good for telling and improving upon around the bar.

Partaking

Sometimes a guest will leave an impression that continues to emerge long after they are gone. In one case that I will never forget, it was a bright spring morning. The sun gave me so much energy that I decided I would work outdoors, or at least started to. As I headed out the back door to the barn, I looked for some things that needed doing in the yard. As is often the case, things will find me to do rather than me finding things to do. And this morning turned out to be one of those days. As I was walking toward the barn, I surveyed the condition of the yard; it being spring and all, it had not had much attention since the last remnants of winter had melted away. So there was plenty to be done there, but by the time I made it to the barn and slid the door open, the general state of disorganization struck me.

Winter weather—often cold, windy, wet—has a funny way of influencing how the barn gets organized. Often, things just get put away in the nearest available space. Well, the time had come for me to put things in the place they were intended. It was only with the barn organized and every tool in the right place that I could properly attack the yard work.

I started by just taking things out and setting them in the yard with some forethought as to the order in which I would return them. First, I wanted the tabula rasa with which to work my organizational concept of the perfect barn. With the barn about one-third empty, I started to consider a yard sale, when the wind started to pick up. I could hear the wind chimes that hung on the front porch peal the alarm, as some of the lighter inventory collected on the lawn started to move under the influence of the wind. Then I felt the first fat, warm raindrops hit me. This was followed by a flash of lightning and, almost immediately, by a crash of thunder that roared in my ears and was too close to the flash of light. The wind whipped harder, and the rain started to come at me sideways. I looked into the sky through squinting eyes, and it had turned completely black on the horizon, and the clouds were rolling in over me, swirling like black ink. Again, lightning and an immediate crash of thunder. The wife came out, the screen door at the back of the house nearly unhinged by the wind, and in about three minutes, we managed to pile back in the barn what had taken thirty minutes to get out. And it looked about the same as when I had started.

I got myself back in the house while outside the rain and wind raged. The storm had come so suddenly, so violently, and with a fury that was frightening. The course of things now disrupted, I moved to the front room, or parlor as the wife likes to call it. There, I found a man sitting in the chair on one side of the fireplace. There was no fire in the fireplace, but he looked as warm and comfortable, reading a newspaper, as if there were. Perhaps it was his calm in contrast to the storm outside that contributed to this sense. In the haste of our organizing, the wife must have forgotten to tell me we had a new guest. Toweling her hands and rearranging her wind-tossed hair, she sought to rectify the situation, saying, "This is Mr. James Frank."

I introduced myself, shaking his hand.

He said, "Briggs. You may call me Briggs."

Curious, I asked, "How did you come by that name?"

"Which?" he asked. "James, Frank, or Briggs?"

"Briggs, I guess," I said, realizing that my question might have seemed impertinent.

"It's my middle name, but those who know me use it."

He smiled, I smiled, and he returned to his paper.

I asked, "Would you like a fire?"

"No, I'm comfortable as is, but if you would like to start one to dry yourself, don't hold back on my account." Again, he smiled and returned to his paper.

I took his body language to mean that he was content to be left alone, and I figured since I had apparently escaped being rude, I would quit while I was ahead. Besides, something else was about to find me to do. I noticed that the books on the shelves on either side of the fireplace were leaning in various directions, some on their side, some with the spine showing titles upside down, as if the grandchildren had recently visited. Maybe the wife forgot to tell me they were here too. I set about to put order to the books on the left side of the room facing the fireplace but decided not to address the same need on the other side because I would have been working at Briggs's back.

On the table, next to the chair, sitting on the left side of the fireplace across from Briggs, there was a copy of the Holy Bible. It looked as if something was stuffed in between its pages, so I picked it up and sat down in the chair. I opened the book to the first insert, which turned out to be a maple leaf, and found that it marked the fifty-first Psalm, "The Miserere: Prayer of Repentance." I read it. It reminded me of the Act of Contrition we had to memorize when we made our first penance. Yes, I had been to confession since the first time; but admittedly, it's been more years since the last confession than it took to make my first. I do know I would struggle to start today. "Bless me, Father, for I have sinned. My last confession was _______." Anyhow, reading this gave me more peace than disruption, so I started to turn the pages to the next insert. I noticed Briggs glance up from his paper in my direction.

Here, I came to the Book of Job, chapter 28, "The Inaccessibility of Wisdom." This was not the only chapter on the page, but it drew my interest. I did not feel a particular need for repentance, but I'd long acknowledged that I was short on wisdom. This page was marked by an oak leaf. I read it. I was struck by the last lines of the chapter: "Behold, the fear of the Lord is wisdom: and avoiding evil is understanding." Now I began to wonder if maple and oak had anything to do with the other. It seemed you could only repent after you had failed to avoid evil by failing to understand. That would seem to be a lack of wisdom, which Job tells us is fear of the Lord.

"Briggs?" I asked.

"Yes, sir?" he replied, looking away from his paper and to me.

"Have you done much reading of the Bible?"

"I am familiar with the book."

"What does fear of the Lord mean to you?"

"To me? Well, the Lord is a particular thing, so fear of the Lord is going to be a particular fear."

"How so?"

"Usually, fear for me is a feeling I get when I am in the presence of something I would rather avoid. Like I have a fear of heights, so if I were standing on the roof, I would feel some anxiety. The anxiety being caused by being afraid that I might fall and come to some harm."

"I get that. For some reason, I am afraid of bats. One time we had one come down that very chimney and fly around this room. Though I run close to 180 pounds, this thing weighing a few ounces scared the hell out of me."

"Those are both examples of what I would call servile fears. They have a power over us because of the harm we sense they could cause to us."

"Uh-huh," I said, betraying a vague understanding.

"Now if we speak of the Lord, and I know this will mean different things to different people, he is different as a thing we don't necessarily want to avoid. Quite the opposite, most folk I know seek to be in the Lord's presence. Moreover, we do not think of the Lord as someone or something that will cause us harm."

"I'm with you."

"So for me, fear of the Lord is different. It has this sense of awe, being overwhelmed in the presence of the Lord for sure. But more importantly, it is a reverence of or an anxiety of doing harm to the Lord that is the fear of the Lord. Like a child who fears they will disappoint their parent, let them down, somehow earn their disapproval. That sort of thing. I call this filial fear."

We sat in silence for a while, and I thought on what Briggs had to say. It took a while, but it made sense. A wise person would want to remain in the presence and favor of the Lord and fear losing this. Understanding how to do this is as simple as avoiding evil. But if you fail to avoid evil, repentance is the way to restore yourself to the Lord's presence. This reminded me of the story about little Johnny who prayed and prayed that God would give him a bike. The bike never came. So one day, Johnny stole a bike. Now he knew this was not an answer to his prayers, so the next day, he went to penance to confess his sin, and all was made right.

"Briggs?" I interrupted the silence.

"Yes, sir?"

"It doesn't look like this storm is going to let up. I was thinking I might have a sip of Jameson. Care to join me?"

"Not sure that I would care for some whiskey, but I will join you in a cup of coffee."

We got up from our chairs and walked to the dining room, turned right, and went into the bar. I hollered to the wife, who was in the kitchen, "Do we have any coffee on?"

"Yes. You want a cup?"

"Make it two. Briggs would like one too." I turned to Briggs. "How do you like yours, Briggs?"

"Black."

"Make them both black," I shouted.

We sat down, and I found my bottle of Jameson and poured an ounce or two into a glass. I offered again a pour to Briggs; he smiled and waved me off. Just after having taken my first sip, the wife came in with two cups of coffee, steam swirling off the top of them. The aroma arrived just as she set them on the bar in front of us. She looked at me, concerned; I thought sternly, *Perhaps she's expressing her disapproval of my whiskey.* She said, "Can I see you a minute?"

"Sure," I replied, and we stepped out of the bar into the dining room.

She whispered, "His name is James Frank, not Briggs."

"Okay, thanks," I whispered back and returned to the bar.

Briggs was sipping at his coffee, replacing it on the bar, and I asked, "You sure you don't want some milk or sugar?"

"No, thanks. Got used to taking my coffee black in the Navy, but I may take you up on a shot of the whiskey if you are willing to pour it into my coffee."

I pushed the bottle toward him. "Help yourself. So you were in the Navy?"

He poured a good measure. "Yes, for about ten years, then I left and joined the Merchant Marine. Stayed in there for about another twenty, twenty-three years to be exact. Anyhow, one day I went to the galley to get a cup of coffee. And as I was pouring the powdered creamer into my coffee, along with it came a big old cockroach. That's the last time I drank my coffee with creamer, or anything else for that matter."

"Except whiskey."

"Yes, sir."

"So what brings you to town?"

"Well, earlier you asked me how I came by my name, and in a sense, it has something to do with that. Do you know of Frederick Douglass?"

"I know of him, but not a lot. I know he escaped from slavery and was a minister and famous for his speeches. In fact, he gave a speech once, not far from here, in Elmira. I've been to the place he gave that speech."

"Well, that's pretty good, and here is where the connection is: when Frederick Douglass escaped from slavery, he went to New Bedford, Massachusetts. Among his friends was an ancient relative of mine, John Briggs, whom he mentions in his autobiography. At the time, Frederick Douglass was not anyone famous. But in time, he did become prominent, and members of my family were proud of their association. From that time on, any of the progeny of Briggs who did not have the surname Briggs was given a middle name of Briggs. That's how I came by the name."

"So what brings you to town?"

I took another pour of whiskey. Briggs did the same; this time with no coffee to dilute it.

"Yes, well, after thirty-three years at sea and no place other than a few ports to call home, I decided to look into my past and my family history. John Briggs is as far back as I can get, so he is sort of a bookend. See, he was born into slavery and, like Douglass, escaped. I find it funny that likely his real name was not Briggs. Douglass's family name was Bailey when he escaped, but like most former slaves, they took on new names to conceal themselves from bounty hunters.

But some of John Briggs's family did come this way a couple of generations later, and it is here my search has brought me."

"That's interesting. Though I have to tell you the only person I know who goes by Briggs is a guy I know from my friend Walt's gas station. But he's a White guy, so I'm pretty sure he isn't related."

"Don't be so sure. Despite appearances, I'm a White guy too, at least in part. Maybe your Briggs is just a Black guy who looks White. In any case, remember, my name is James Frank. I just go by Briggs because too many people got confused not knowing which was my first and which was my last name."

"So what have you found so far about your family?"

"Not much that is interesting. I know, of course, about my nearest relatives. My mom and dad neither had more than a high school education. My dad was in the Navy too, enlisted out of high school. He served before and during the Korean War. In 1948, Truman had desegregated the military, so Black men were not limited to being steward's mates. He was a regular rated seaman and worked below decks, a boiler technician. Finished as a petty officer, second class. The best thing about his experience was that he learned enough about keeping a turbine going that he was able to find a job working in a power plant, which he did for forty years.

"He always spoke with pride about his time in the Navy, not so much about his service though. That was a big reason for me joining. I was a fairly good athlete in high school, but not good enough to get a scholarship. However, the Navy offered me the opportunity to get a degree through the ROTC program. I took advantage of that and earned a bachelor's degree in mechanical engineering and a commission as an officer. Dad was proud of that. As I said, I spent ten years, made the rank of lieutenant commander, and decided I would do better in the Merchant Marine."

"It seems both you and your dad benefited from your time in the Navy."

"In a sense, yes. We both learned a skill from which we could earn a living. I can't speak for my dad, but I can tell you I learned an even greater thing from the sea."

"What was that?"

"The sea is a vast thing. When you are at sea, way off from land, in every direction you look, you can see the curvature of the earth but nothing beyond the horizon. You can see where night meets day. As a particular individual, you loosen your sense of self. You partake in the vastness of the sea that you touch. You and the sea meet, like the water and the sky at the horizon, like the light and dark of day and night. It's the same with a ship's captain and its men. They are bound together on the vast sea through the ship that carries them."

"I've felt that way when I am fishing, wading in a stream, with a fish on. But it's not that way all the time."

"Sad and true. I've learned that for most of my ancestors, life has not been that way."

"How do you mean?"

"Go back to John Briggs. He was born into slavery. For the first twenty years or so of his life, he was property. He was birthed but did not know his mother or father, sold, separated from family and the communities in which he passed time, and put in the field to labor not for his own benefit or subsistence but, like a beast, for the benefit of his owner. He escaped from that and was free in the sense that his labor now was for his benefit, or at least represented an exchange of what another wanted of him for what he wanted of another. But he wasn't free yet. He could not take passage on trains or boats except in segregated areas. He was denied access to public places for entertainment or instruction. Because of his limited skill and learning, he was only capable of the most menial kinds of work that afforded at best a subsistence wage and no opportunity to accumulate any capital."

"I guess he did not feel much that he was partaking in the land or country he was touching."

"No, sir. And it didn't get much better for the next several generations. His daughter married William Frank. He was a liberated slave who fought for the Union during the Civil War and, after the war, returned to the south to claim his forty acres and a mule and to do the only thing he knew how to do: farm. Well, the promise of a land grant was broken. Most of the land was going back to the prewar owners. William faced the alternative of being arrested for vagrancy and forced into labor or tenant farming. He was able to work some land for his own subsistence but, again lacking any capital, had to borrow for equipment and seed. By the time he harvested his crop and surrendered what was needed to retire his debt, owing to the vagaries of nature, in many years, there was nothing left. In some years, the only harvest was a portion of unpaid debt. Yes, the law had freed William from chattel slavery and put him into debt servitude.

"Moreover, while legally free, he was still not able to partake of the fruits of his freedom. He still did not have access to public venues for rest, food, entertainment, or learning. Nor was he allowed to cast a vote in political matters. His children were able to access segregated schools, but only when they could afford to be away from the work needed to be done on the farm."

"So why didn't he just leave, go where he would not be other, have some opportunity in life?"

"Go where? They were born here. There was no place to go where they would not be other."

I didn't have an answer. It just seems people come and go these days. But I didn't really know what they found when they got there.

"Besides, this country had just spilled out its blood to stay united, and the emancipation of the enslaved into such a country seemed the best opportunity. So they stayed. Generation after generation, they worked. They grew crops and, eventually, some capital too. They became landowners, got education, got to vote, took a role in government. We fought in wars, but sadly, I still don't feel we partake in the opportunity that is in this country."

"Hmm."

"At sea, a captain partakes in the crew, the crew partakes in the ship, the ship partakes in the sea, the sea connects to the sky, the night to the day. All are connected. All partake in the other."

Silence was the only answer I could summon.

"Thanks for the drink and the conversation. I think I'll go to my room to rest for a while."

"Aye, aye, Briggs."

He smiled and left the room.

Buck and Dot

It was early days; we had been operating as a boarding house for about a year and recently had refurbished the third floor. We were just building a little bit of a following, even had a few repeat guests, but were rarely sold out. So when the wife's cousin contacted us to take in Buck and Dot, despite all knowing what was coming, we were hard-pressed to say no.

What was coming was that Buck, approaching his ninth decade, had been diagnosed with cancer. He had been treated and lived with it for several years, but now it was getting the better of him, and he needed more care and attention than Dot could provide on her own at their home on the far outskirts of town. Their children and spouses were all full-time working, some in the business Buck had started, so they could not devote the time needed to this level of care. We are a close family, so this solution made a lot of sense given our situation with the boarding house.

So we moved Buck and Dot up to the third floor. Despite being accessible only by the stair, all agreed this would be best, as it would leave them undisturbed by the comings and goings of whatever other guests we might get. And Buck was still well enough that he could get up and down the stairs for meals and whatever socializing he wanted or needed.

No one had a clear idea what the duration of Buck's stay would be. We met with the hospice folk to prepare to take him in. Among other things, they told us to prepare us for the demands and emotional toll of being a caretaker; they gave guidance on how to keep him comfortable as he approached his final days. One of the things they told us was that he might lose consciousness or appear to, but it was nonetheless important for us, as well as him, that we, someone of us, be there in his last moments. Another thing they instructed us on was that if he was in some discomfort, we could slip a pill—it was a white pill—under his tongue, and this would make his passing easier. This wasn't a Kevorkian remedy, only a sedative and pain reliever. But I'm not sure Dot fully understood this.

Well, as it came to pass, on more than several occasions, we were able to put this counsel into operation. On one such occasion, it was a pleasant spring day; the trees were at that stage between budding and turning out their leaves. Late March or early April if I recall correctly. There was a breeze that pushed a warm air around and chased away the chill still held by the earth and our bones. It was warm enough that we opened the windows and let the air circulate through the house. Buck had stayed down in the parlor after lunch and was enjoying the day sitting and talking with Dot and anyone else who made their way through the room.

Around about two thirty in the afternoon, Buck stood and started to make his way up the stairs. As he made his way up the stairs, he announced, "Feeling a little tired." He paused and then added, "Guess I'll take a nap."

Dot followed shortly after, no doubt to make him comfortable and just to be with him. Just in case, as we had been advised. It was with a little bit of sadness the wife and I watched her ascend after Buck. Not with any sense of premonition of what would be next, just with a shared sense or awareness of what might happen.

Around three fifteen, we heard Dot coming quietly down the stairs. She made her way into the living room, sat in a large armchair, rested her chin on her palm, and stared out the window. I observed her from the kitchen through the dining room; she was just sitting there quietly and convulsing gently. I went to the wife and told her what I saw and thought that she should go and see if Dot was okay.

She did, approaching her quietly, placing her hand on her shoulder, and bending to speak softly to her. The wife returned to a standing position then turned to me, signaling for me to come into the room. I approached with some haste, still uncertain of what had happened.

I asked, "Is everything okay, Dot?"

"Oh yes." It seemed that Dot had tears in her eyes.

"And Buck?"

"Yes, him too." And after taking a breath, she added, "I thought it was the end. He lay down, and in about three minutes, he was lying so quietly I thought he had passed. Well, I reached for my Bible and opened it to the twenty-third Psalm and started reading it to myself. I was just trying to find peace in what was happening. I got through it once and started again. It's a short one, you know. I felt the cadence of the Psalm become the cadence of my breathing, and this was keeping me calm. And just then, Buck started snoring. Well, with such a reversal of my understanding, I was shocked. I couldn't find a Psalm for what I was feeling, and his snoring was so loud it now had overtaken the cadence of my breathing, so I came downstairs to gather my thoughts."

"Well, it's just that I saw you sitting here quietly, and I thought you were crying a bit because I saw your shoulders shaking."

"I guess I was both crying and laughing. A little of both, but nothing to worry about."

So we all went back to what we were doing. Nothing to see here. I guess just a close call to what was on our mind, but little to do with reality.

The second occasion came about three weeks later. This time it was at night. Everyone had gone to, and had been in, bed for the night. It was about 1:00 a.m. when, for some reason, I woke up. Looking out toward the kitchen from our bedroom, I sensed a light on in the house, probably the front parlor. At the time, we had two guests in the house. They had both been in for dinner, and neither one had gone out after. It wasn't unusual for someone to come down into the parlor after the house had bedded down. I thought someone just forgot to turn out the light. In any event, I knew I was not going to get back to sleep until I ran this whole thing to ground. So I got up, put on my pajama pants (I keep them hanging on the bedpost just for such occasions), and made my way through the kitchen on the way to the living room to investigate.

Again, I saw Dot sitting in the chair just as I had a few weeks ago. The thoughts—more specifically, the context of that memory came back to me, and I was filled with the dread I had felt then. This time I made my way quietly to Dot. She heard me walk into the room and turned to face me.

"Sorry if I woke you," she said.

"Is everything okay?" I said.

"Oh yes, fine. It happened again though. Kind of. We were just sleeping. Buck was a little restless, not unusually so though, not even so much as to keep me awake. But then he went very quiet, enough so that it was that that woke me. I was listening very carefully but could not hear him breathing. So I got up, went to my chair, turned on the lamp, and said a prayer. The lamp cast its light weakly on Buck, and I sensed no movement, nor did I hear him breathing. I reached for my Bible and opened it, again reading from the twenty-third Psalm. On my second pass, I fell into the cadence of the Psalm. And by the time I was at the third verse, I started to read out loud. And just as I started the sixth verse, I heard his voice: 'Dot!' Startled, I looked at Buck, and he was propped up on his elbows. He said, 'What the hell is that you're reading? Come back to bed.' I turned off the lamp, and before the light was out, Buck was back asleep, not a care in the world. So I just came down here where I could sit in peace."

"Well, then, Dot, I guess I'll just leave you in peace."

She just nodded and smiled as I turned to walk back to my bed.

The third such occasion, but not the final, was later in the year. If I recall, it was in the autumn; the leaves were turning but not falling much yet. Maybe we had just got more accustomed to Buck's circadian rhythms, but the summer seemed to involve a little less of knocking on heaven's door. Anyhow, it was a September day, I think, and Buck was heading up for what had become his customary nap, Dot not far behind.

The second floor was full, and everyone was going to be in for dinner, so the wife and I were in the kitchen planning the meal that we usually served around 7:00 p.m. It was sometime after three when

Dot came down and joined us in the kitchen. She didn't say anything, and she seemed to be at peace, perhaps more pensive. I was drinking coffee. Dot made herself a cup of tea and sat down at the kitchen table. She still hadn't said anything; so the wife, who suffers from a horror of silence, asked her, "Dot, what's on your mind?"

"Well, Buck had a hard time settling down. He seemed agitated and could not get comfortable. He was only half asleep, and I decided that it was time to use one of the pills the hospice had given us. So I put one in his mouth, and within a couple of minutes, he settled down and fell asleep."

The wife and I just looked at each other.

"How long ago was this, Dot?" I asked.

"Oh, about a half hour ago. I waited about fifteen minutes before I came down."

"And?" the wife prompted.

"And I just don't know if this is finally it. I'm not prepared to make my way back upstairs to get my answer. But I guess if it is, I am at peace with it. I just don't know how I feel about hastening it with that pill."

"Dot, the hospice told us the pill wouldn't bring about anything but only ease what was going to happen anyhow," the wife asserted.

"Well, I took that to mean whatever makes it easier means just that: it makes it easier. I don't want to make Buck's end come any easier, but I'm afraid I have."

"Oh, dear, I don't think you understand."

"Will you pray with me?" Dot pleaded.

"Of course, we will" came our response in unity.

So we prayed. I don't recall the exact words, but the gist of it was that we prayed for the strength to understand and accept God's will in this and asked that God would lift up Buck who we felt lived his life honoring God by living as God had asked us and shown us through his Son, Jesus Christ. Then we got to discussing how we could best honor Buck. We pretty much settled on the way Buck approached most things in life; he was not timid, never shied away from a challenge, and if given the choice, went for the big portion in life. Sometimes his enthusiasm carried him beyond his abilities, but never in a way that intended or caused harm to those around him. We all said we would try to honor Buck by living this way so the world wouldn't miss him as much. I wish we had recorded it.

Without noticing, we had just spent the better part of two hours eulogizing Buck, and it was past 5:30 p.m. I offered to go check on Buck. But Dot said, "No, I'll go do it."

As she got up to walk out of the kitchen, she stopped, and in walked Buck, asking, "What's for dinner? I'm hungry."

Dot set the table for dinner that night, and I noticed that at each place setting she had set out a large spoon. We weren't having soup, but I didn't ask why. I'm sure now that it was just an homage to Buck.

Matilda's Christmas

It was the first Christmas that our son, his wife, and their two children joined us at home, the boarding house. Nellie, the baby, was in bed; and Matilda—I call her Tilly—the four-year-old, was sitting in my lap. She got up and pulled a book from one of the family's bags, Clement C. Moore's *The Night Before Christmas*, climbed back into my lap, and commanded, "Read." Now I enjoy looking at the Christmas tree with a fire going in the fireplace. The warmth of the fire with its glow combining with that of the tree and the scent of the tree mixing with a hint of smokiness from the fire create a delicious memory. Lost in a memory, I turned my attention to Tilly and said, "Let me tell you a story about that book." She smiled and said, "Okay."

"I remember when I was a child, about your age. It was Christmas Eve. Everyone had long been in bed. I went downstairs and plugged in the Christmas tree. I did not turn on any other lights. The fire had gone out, with only gray and a faint orange glow of the last embers in the hearth. The smoky scent was still there to mingle with the Christmas tree. I had lain down on the couch, staring at the tree, and must have fallen asleep.

"I was startled awake by a noise that sounded as if it came from the roof, and when I looked over to the fireplace, I saw a black boot pushing down. It was followed by another, and then a big butt started to back out of the fireplace. I knew instantly who this was. He had on his red suit, dusted with soot that was black, and on his back, flung over his shoulder, he carried his sack. He turned around to see me staring at him, and when our eyes met, his lit up with surprise. I looked deeply into his eyes, which by now were smiling at me. Now I don't recall that he spoke at all, but I am certain he told me this story. I was still thinking of the noise on the roof, wondering what it was, and seeing Santa answered the question. I knew it was Santa's reindeer. Santa must have seen this in my eyes, prompting him to tell me how he got his reindeer. Santa told me, 'It was a cold, dry day. The sky was bright blue without a single cloud. With every breath, I could make my own little clouds form in front of me and watch them quickly disappear. It was quiet, as is usual in the early morning. The snow lay out flat, sparkling in silver and light blue, and it crunched as I took each step. At first, the crisp surface resisted the sole of my boot then gave way as my foot submerged into the powdery snow below. The only sounds I heard were the snow crunching, my own breathing, and the beat of my heart.

"'I noticed a spot of red in the sparkling sea of snow that spread before me. As I got closer to the red spot, I also saw that the smooth surface of the snow had been broken by the prints of an animal. I followed the trail of red and the prints that ran alongside. This was a blood trail, and I thought that some poor creature must have been hurt. Even though it was the morning of Christmas Eve and I had plenty of work yet to do, I knew in my heart that I could not leave a hurt creature in the wild. So I decided I would follow the trail to see where it led.

"'Happily, it did not lead far. It was only a few hundred yards to the end of the field where the tree line of a pine forest met the edge of the field. A few more steps into the forest, there was a thick tangle of holly bushes—some with red berries, some without. The red blood trail mixed with the fallen berries and might easily have been lost, except I looked into the holly and saw something that seemed out of place. I saw what looked like naked branches. Then I saw them move. There was no wind to move them, so I looked closer and started to wade into the prickly holly. What I found there did not make me happy.

"'Lying in the cover of the holly was a beautiful, strong, and ancient reindeer. The reindeer had been shot by a hunter whose aim or bullet failed to do its job. I was overtaken by sadness. I knelt to comfort the reindeer and stroke his fur. He had a great white chest and tail. The rest of his fur was a gradient of gray that had a few flecks of the reddish rust-colored fur of his youth. The reindeer looked into my eyes, and I could sense that life was escaping him, and unless I did something, this would be the end for the reindeer. I passed my hand gently over the wound, and a flash as bright as lightning filled the stand of holly. I was momentarily blinded and knocked back off my feet.

"'When I regained my sight, what I saw was wondrous and lifted my spirits. The ancient reindeer was on his feet, hale and ready to bolt off. But the reindeer did not bolt. He looked back at me. Again, his eyes told me that he was grateful and wanted to repay the kindness I had shown and gift of life I had given him. Then I saw his eyes say, "Watch this," and the reindeer did bolt. With the speed of lightning, in three steps, he took to the air. Again, space was filled with the flash that had accompanied my healing touch. The reindeer flew out of the forest. I ran after him and saw him circling above the field that I had walked through to find him. The reindeer then landed and stood by me and again looked into my eyes.

"'As we stood there, the reindeer's gaze into my eyes was suddenly broken as he turned his attention abruptly to stare intently into the woods. The reindeer must have heard it first, but now I could hear it—a distant bleat and the crashing of something large rushing through the woods. I had no idea what was coming, but I could tell it would be here soon. Fulfilling my expectations, with a mighty crash, another reindeer burst from the forest. Into the field he ran at full speed, heading directly toward me. He came to a stop within a foot of me, when the flurry of snow that trailed the reindeer overtook us, covering us all with a powdery dusting of snow. As the snow was settling, the reindeer let out a mighty bleat that sounded like thunder.

"'I could see that these two reindeer were nearly identical. I could see from the look in their eyes they were happy to see each other and, indeed, were brothers. I knew I would not be able to tell them apart, so I decided I had better give them names. Laying my hands on the first, I named him Blixem because of the bright flash that accompanied his flight. And again laying my hands on the second, I named him Dunder because of the noise that announced his arrival. Then to my surprise, both reindeer started to run. And with a flash of lightning and a bleat of thunder, they took to the air to again circle the field high over my head. Clearly, some of the Christmas magic that I had been given long ago had been transferred to the reindeer. As I watched them circle, I realized that the sun was now high in the sky and that I had fallen terribly behind in my work, for Christmas Eve was near. I had an idea.

"'I rushed home, Blixem and Dunder following me in flight. As I approached home, I could see my helpers were already engaged in loading my sleigh. But then there was a burst of lightning and a crash of thunder, and they stopped and looked in the sky in wonder. How could there be a storm without a cloud in the sky on such a cold winter day? Then they saw the reindeer flying in the sky, and below I was running with a rooster tail of snow rising behind me. At first, they perceived that I was being chased by the reindeer and rushed toward me to protect me from this odd attack. But they were confused, because not only had they never seen me running so fast but they had also never seen reindeer that fly. This whole scene caused such a commotion and confusion and considerable anxiety to Momma Claus—I call her that though she is my wife—that I resolved that from that day forward I would only touch the reindeer on Christmas, so that is why it is the only day they can fly.

"'By now, it had got really late. I was way behind and had to leave to start delivering presents to the children. The idea that had struck me in the field was to hitch the deer to the sleigh so that I could move a little faster and make up the time I had lost. So I asked one of my helpers to make it so. I also had a couple of them hop into the sleigh with me so they could wrap presents as I made my rounds. With Blixem and Dunder hitched and a couple of my helpers on the sleigh, I once again laid my hands on the reindeer, flung myself into the sleigh, and with a flash and a crash, we took to the air.'

"This was the first Christmas that reindeer pulled Santa's sleigh, and in some places, gifts were left unwrapped, sometimes just stuffed in stockings, because Blixem and Dunder were so fast Santa's helpers could not get all the presents wrapped. Now in later years, both Blixem and Dunder had baby reindeer, which by their second year were strong enough to pull the sleigh. The most reindeer that Santa had pull his sleigh was eight, except for one year. We know the name of those eight reindeer because Santa had told this same story to a fellow named Clement C. Moore years before, and he wrote this poem in which they are mentioned. I think I can find that part of the poem. Here it is:

> 'When, what to my wondering eyes should appear,
> but a miniature sleigh, and eight tiny reindeer,
> with a little old driver, so lively and quick,
> I knew in a moment it must be St. Nick.
>
> More rapid than eagles his coursers they came,
> And he whistled, and shouted, and call'd them by name:
> "Now, Dasher! Now, Dancer! Now, Prancer, and Vixen!
> "On, Comet! On, Cupid! On, Donder and Blitzen!
>
> "To the top of the porch! To the top of the wall!
> "Now dash away! Dash away! Dash away all!"'

"Moore called Santa's first reindeer Donder and Blitzen in his poem. That's because he spoke English. Now as I said, Santa never spoke a word. All this was communicated through the look in his eyes, and I am pretty sure he called them Dunder and Blixem, using the old Dutch language in which he must have been thinking. And surprisingly, I understood. The one time Santa used nine reindeer—and we all know this story—was when it was a particularly foggy Christmas Eve, and he added Rudolph to the team that night."

I looked at Tilly in my lap, and she was fast asleep. I carried Tilly upstairs to her room. As I entered the room, I must have wakened my son who was asleep in a chair next to the baby's crib. He smiled and rose to pull back the blankets on Tilly's bed. We tucked her in and stealthily retreated from the room. I started down the stairs since I had left on the lights and wanted to make the rounds to secure things before we settled into bed. My son followed, sat down, sighed, and seemed to want to just take in the bouquet of the fire, tree, its lights, and the quiet that descends at night. I laughed inside in appreciation. So I did the same, taking up the spot I was earlier sitting in with Tilly.

"They're really special," he said.

"Who are?" I asked, not certain to what he was referring.

"The kids."

"Yeah, I know it. Had a few myself."

"Funny how your perspective changes with kids. I can remember Christmas as a kid, and I think of it now. It still has some of the magic that filled the imagination, but it's also fun to see your own kids experiencing it."

"That's one benefit of kids. They allow you to be a kid again. Not only the memories, but if you're smart, you can get away with acting like a kid. Even when someone else is watching."

"Ha, and on the other hand, I've noticed as Matilda is getting older, when I find myself laughing at something she's done or said, I sometimes find I'm laughing at myself. So who's being who?"

Again, I laughed internally. "Yeah, we end up giving quite a bit to each other. I remember when you were born and I held you in my arms for the first time. I looked at you and felt so much love for you, wanted all the very best for you, and was committed to you. But you know what you gave me back?"

My son sat silently, thinking about how to respond. I'm sure he was wondering, *Is this a trick question?*

"No, what was that?"

"It was the first time I realized how my father felt about me, and it changed the way I felt about him."

Eternity

One day, while fishing the creek, I lost track of time. Like when one moment passes into the next so that you do not notice them passing at all. And I found myself at the lake. It must have been some time after eight in the evening; the sun was well into its retreat to the west. So I sat on the beach and thought I would hang out for the sunset. As I sat there, I got lost in the rhythm of the waves washing up on the shore and got to thinking about them. How the water rises and becomes salient on the lake—sometimes as whitecaps, pushed along by the wind—and then crashes and collapses along the shore to return to the lake, no longer discrete.

As my thoughts revisited the day and some of the memories I carried into it, there was one that stuck with me. This particular memory was from back in my childhood and ends where my day started. Maybe that's why it surfaced. There was this fellow, Terry— Terry Toggle we called him out of earshot. This wasn't a pejorative, more of a handle that testified to his tinkering and being handy with things. Terry had some developmental challenges. The story went that his cord wrapped around his neck at birth and cut off his air for too long. I don't know the truth of it, and as a kid, I did not fully understand this explanation and was not all that curious. Though today I understand it. Terry was already an adult when I came to know him, and he made his way around town on an old Schwinn 3-speed. He lived with his grandmother, and again, as kids, we were content with not knowing anything of the gap left by his parents' absence.

As I mentioned, Terry was a grown man when I came to know him; and while we crossed paths in town, I and the other kids did not have a lot to do with him. He always was two to five days away from being clean-shaven and had a Marlboro cigarette permanently dangling from his lip with smoke circling his head. That his brand was Marlboro became known to us, as he often discarded his empty packs in his trail and carried on like he was a cowboy, hat and all, the real Marlboro man. His hands were dirty with grease and grit ground into his digits and under his nails. The first two fingers and thumb of his right hand were stained yellow from tobacco. Though I swear I never saw him without that cigarette in his mouth.

He often had one of those white Styrofoam to-go cups—I presume charged with coffee—and this was a frequent offering that adults would approach him with, spending a few minutes to converse. Like I said, as kids, we didn't have much to do with him. Not that he was dangerous, but he always seemed a bit nervous around us. Whenever we got even a little close, he would start cranking with this thumb on the bell attached to his handlebars, whether he was moving or not. So we just steered clear of him.

Terry had a small cart that he rigged to his bike that he pulled behind him as a trailer of sorts. As I mentioned, Terry was handy, and people in town would give him things that needed repairing—anything, from toasters to lawn mowers, power, and push. He'd also take your knives, hedge clippers, or scissors and put a sharp edge on the blades. Sometimes people would send Terry to the store to pick things up for them, maybe cigarettes from the corner store, some bread and milk from the grocery store, or some other item from the hardware store.

This was a combination of Terry providing a useful and helpful service and some people giving Terry something to do and justifying giving him a small financial reward for his efforts. Terry was a fixture in town, and his regularity and reliability came to be something that many became dependent upon or at least appreciated.

One day, Terry's arrival was preceded by a clacking racket. Terry had resurrected what all kids had at one time done, the old trick of clipping a playing card to the fork so that it would flick against the spokes of the wheel. Well, if that was not enough to get your attention, what you saw when you turned to the source of the noise held your attention. Terry had mounted on his cart what looked to be a chest of drawers. Moreover, he had mounted onto the frame of his bike a small motor that could assist him in pulling this added weight. It turned out that the library was doing a renovation, and among the things renovated were the drawers that held all the index cards that embodied the wisdom of the Dewey decimal system. Upon closer inspection, it became apparent that the library had replaced some map drawers as well, as a set of four of these formed the base to this rig.

To Terry's mind, this was the perfect rig to carry an essential inventory of the small items that he was often sent off to fetch at a variety of stores and to boot a few of his tools to make small repairs on site. No one seemed to mind paying a nickel or a dime more—Terry's markup—for a small item that sold for less than a dollar had you made the trip to the store. On larger items, very often it was the markup and keep the change. So Terry did all right in his retail operation and seemed to do well in managing his inventory—no perishable items, of course.

On his service and repair business, he did even better. He kept some whetstones and files to keep all manner of cutting things sharp. He could do small engine repairs, gas and electric, with the tools he carried while you wait. Though for some, he might have to take them home for a day or two. He even offered some specialty services like fishing reel repairs and maintenance. I wish we still had him around.

And that's the thing, like the waves rolling into the shore, one day Terry just disappeared. His bike—cart and all—was seen in the parking lot of the fire department one morning. The fire department was in the center of town alongside the creek, right where I started my day. By nighttime, when Terry hadn't showed up and no one had seen him that day, one of the volunteer firemen went over to his grandmother's home to check in. I guess no one had realized it, but she was frail and not of full presence of mind. When asked about Terry or his whereabouts, she had no idea. That night, they wheeled his bike and cart into the fire hall, and that was the last I ever saw of it.

By now, the sun had set, and the waves were still rolling in. I got up and started walking back toward home. If I followed the streets rather than the creek, it was about four miles, an hour plus at a fast pace. By the time I reached the first watering hole, I went in, ordered a beer, and called the wife; and she came to pick me up. When I got in the car, she asked, "What kept you so long?"

Since she did not grow up in town, she had no remembrance of Terry; and my recollections, at this point, were more like a dream that was vivid but hard to talk about in a coherent way. So I answered, "I was just fishing, and when I finished up at the lake, I thought I would stay for the sunset."

She nodded; we had shared that experience enough that no more needed to be said.

Haunting

When I was eleven until I turned fourteen, in the summer we would set up camp on the creek; and depending on our parents, we would spend nights at camp. The usual thing involved a tent, or one year we built a shelter, something like a lean-to with three sides. Most of our food was brought in, a pack of hot dogs and rolls from home, a couple of cans of pop, a bag of pretzels and chips. And the dogs were cooked over a fire that would stay lit until the last one fell asleep. It was not that we would take up residence at the camp; we would be in and out of our homes during the day, mainly to resupply or use the toilet if we got tired of wiping with leaves. Parents didn't seem to worry too much then.

That was until that last year. That was the year Bobby McKinnon was killed on the creek. He was a year younger than me—only thirteen, maybe twelve—and he wasn't part of our four- to six-man camping cohort. In fact, he wasn't even camping; his parents wouldn't let him. It was his parents who found him. He had not come home, and they went looking for him. When they found him dead, he was lying on the bank of the creek, shoes off, his legs below the knees in the water. I know this much because when the police arrived, we got close enough to see. What we did not see and only heard about later was that his head was split and there was a bloody rock lying about three feet away. Suspicious, they called it. Suspicion is an invitation to imagination, and before long, we were all well convinced that it was the most brutal of murders.

Of course, we were questioned by the police, as our camp was only about a quarter mile from the scene. Their questions were mostly about if and when we last saw Bobby, was there anyone with him, along that line, trying to piece things together. We had seen him and two or three other guys; in fact, Tad was one of them. But that was earlier in the day, and nothing we saw portended what would happen. As it turned out, what happened was never fully resolved and remains a mystery even today.

You might wonder what this story has to do with the boarding house or any of the goings-on there. Follow me a few more steps and you will know. I've mentioned several times that I spend some time fishing, and I still fish along this creek. If I walk from town all the way down to the lake, I'll pass the site of our camp that year and then the spot where they found Bobby's body. You can still see remnants of the lean-to we built from fallen logs and limbs. And when I come to the spot where they found Bobby, I still get a visceral reaction, like the goose bump feeling without actual goose bumps. I have only had that same feeling two other times. Once when we were out in Montana, the wife and I stopped at the site of Custer's last stand, or the Battle of the Greasy Grass. The site is scattered with markers where soldiers and native people fell. Some of the markers have names on them; others are just marked unknown. Just the sight of all these markers where men had lain and the sense you were walking on soil that had soaked up so much blood caused this same feeling. It was as if you were standing among them. The other time was visiting Omaha Beach in Normandy, France—a place where so much life was lost. While the memorial presentation there is more formal, it was a sense of a "brother's blood [that] cries out" (Gen 4:10) that again made my skin tingle.

The other day, as I had on many other occasions, I walked by that spot; before realizing or reflecting on where I was, I felt that feeling rising in me. That feeling triggered my recall, and in a sense, maybe because I could explain the familiar discomfort, I felt less anxious. I was walking slowly along, looking at the creek, when I heard a splash; and as I looked to the source of the sound, I saw the radiating concentric ripples of what I thought must have been a fish that jumped to take a bug hovering above the water. As I pulled out some line, preparing to cast, I walked back to a better position, and a rock bounced in front of me with a smack and skipped a few times before coming to a rest. "Hmm," I muttered, thinking I had kicked the rock and that I needed to be more careful about my footfalls lest I alert the fish.

I threw out my line just upstream from the mental picture I had of the center of the ripples, hoping the fish was still in the vicinity of its last morsel. I let it drift. Nothing. I cast again, a third, and a fourth time. Then I heard another splash, this time downstream, and as I turned toward it, again, all I saw was the water rippling. Then a rock landed right at my feet. This time I was sure I did not kick it. I did not see it in flight but felt certain that it was thrown at me. That anxious feeling rose again in me, this time stronger than ever, as if someone were standing right next to me at my back. I turned, and while no one was there, I still had a powerful sense of a presence. I hightailed it out of there and continued at a lively pace until I got home.

When I got home, I guess I was still showing some signs of being worked up, causing the wife to ask, "What's got you stirred up?"

So I told her about the series of events and then added my speculation that it was Bobby trying to make his presence known. While she was not out-and-out laughing at me, she was doing a poor job of concealing her dismissal of my explanation. It was just that she never had the feeling, neither at Greasy Grass nor at Omaha Beach, that I experienced, so she had no way of relating to the strong signal I was receiving at the creek. She went so far as to suggest it might have been Walt hiding out in the woods and reminded me of the time Timmy chased me from a hanging. I wish I never told her about that.

Later that night, around five thirty, the boys showed up, and we were having a little happy hour. We had a great surprise when around six, my brother-in-law, Chris, and his three sons—Abe, Joe, and Luke—showed up. They lived about two hours away and were traveling through to a farm auction they wanted to attend the next day. I guess Chris had called the wife, but she forgot to tell me. They were staying for dinner and the night. Anyhow, we got to reminiscing about our childhood again and summers on the creek. Of course, Bobby's murder came up, but I had related none of my experience today. For that matter, none of the guys had heard about the goose bump feeling at Greasy and Omaha, so it wasn't worthwhile trying to fill in all that background and risk dismissal once again.

We ended up eating a little bit later than usual, closer to eight, because the wife had to alter plans with Chris and his boys showing up. The alteration turned out to be me grilling some burgers in the backyard, while she made a cucumber, tomato, onion, and olive salad dressed with a little bit of oil, vinegar, and feta cheese. We also had some corn on the cob. Not fancy, but good. While I was cooking the burgers, two ravens were circling over me, and one let loose of a large white-and-black crap that landed on my head, ear, and shoulder. I had never had a run-in with a bird before, unless you count that time I had a fish hooked on and I was fighting it when an osprey decided it was dinnertime. I didn't think the ravens were after my burgers, and judging from the bombing I took, it seemed they had just eaten.

After we had eaten, we sat at the table for a bit, but Chris wanted to get up early, so we all settled in around ten or so. It was sometime after 1:00 a.m. I woke up. I usually sleep with a fan on; I like it for the white noise. But there was a light ticking—not regular like a clock, but occasional—that made its way through the hum of the fan. I got up and walked out to the kitchen. I heard the tick again, but fainter this time. I returned to the bedroom and heard it again. It was something striking the window. I turned on the light, but that was a mistake. The only effect of that was to turn the window into a mirror, reflecting my own image back at me and doing nothing to illuminate whatever was outside. I turned off the light and opened the window about six inches. I turned on the light and, crouching down, looked through the space I had opened. While the outdoors was now illuminated, I still could not see anything. But I did hear something, so I turned off the light and the fan and returned to the window. I pushed it up a few more inches and listened closely.

Then I heard, not clearly, but better. I said, "Who is that?"

An answer came: "I saw you today. Why did you leave me?"

By now the wife was up, on two elbows, squinting at me in the dark, and asked, "What the deuce is going on?"

"Shh!" I urged. "There's someone out there."

I turned back to the window and said, "Who is it?"

"Return to the creek tomorrow" was all that was said.

I called out a few times in a loud whisper, but there was no reply. I reached over and turned on the light; the wife rolled over and turned it off. I turned it on again, and she turned it off.

"I'm sleeping," she insisted.

And that was the end of it. I lay in bed not able to resume sleep as had the wife. While I was lying there, I became aware that while I was feeling some agitation, I did not have the goose bump feeling I had at the creek.

Then came a knocking sound. At first, a shot of adrenaline moved through me, and as I centered on the source of knocking—it was the front door—it subsided. Still a little nervous, I made my way to the front door. Not repeating my previous mistake, I left the light out before looking through the glass at the top of the door. And there I saw standing—in his pajamas, slippers, and a robe—our neighbor Mike.

"Mike? What can I do for you?"

"Well, I was just checking on you. I saw your lights flashing on and off several times, so I thought maybe there was some trouble. That you were signaling me."

"Gee, thanks for that, Mike. No, it's nothing. The wife heard something. I think it was just a mouse. She turned the light on, I turned it off, she turned it on—like that, you know. Sorry to trouble you, but I do appreciate your concern. Thanks a lot."

"Okay then. Good night."

I made my way back to bed and finally found some sleep.

I guess with all the goings-on, I slept a little longer than usual; and by the time I got up for my first cup of coffee, Chris and the boys had already been fed and were on the road. The wife got up, fed them, and saw them off. She let me get a few swallows of coffee down and asked, "What was that last night?"

I told her the events as I saw them, with no speculating this time.

"So are you thinking of going down to the creek today?"

"No," I answered, I guess revealing a little of the speculation left unsaid.

She shrugged, turned, and asked, "Then what's on the agenda for today?"

"Oh, there's a few things that need doing around here. I guess I could get after the barn that I started when that storm hit."

"Yeah, that was only a few weeks back."

"And I suppose I might get to the garden beds, do a little weeding, mow the lawn. Like I said, plenty to do. Besides, it's pretty warm. The fish are getting a little lethargic these days."

I did get after the barn and, over the course of the next week, the rest of the list I had inadvertently made for myself. I guess I was moping around, and the wife made me a nice lunch. While we were sitting there, I wasn't saying much, and she looked at me somewhat sympathetically. I should say I mistook sympathetic for apologetic because she let on that what happened that night was all a ruse. She had told Chris and the boys about what had happened that day and how it spooked me while I was cooking the burgers. The boys then came up with a plan, the wife being in on it, to pull off the scene at our bedroom window. Having learned the truth of that night, I put on my happy face, laughed with my wife, and went fishing.

I purposely walked as far as Bobby's place just to demonstrate, to myself and anyone who might ask, that I was not spooked. Though I will admit that old goose bump feeling rose again as I approached and while I stood there, with my back to the woods, casting upstream.

* * *

That evening when I returned home, I felt a chill and decided to start a fire in the parlor. I poured a Jameson in the bar, returning to the parlor to sit by the fire. The wife walked into the room and said, "I got a call from Tom Doyle today. You remember him? Said he'll be coming through again and will stay for a couple of days."

"Great! Maybe there's more about that woman who went missing."

About the Author

Mitt is a first-time author of fiction who enjoys sitting on the porch, with a cigar and whiskey, listening to a Phillies game on the radio. He believes in God the creator, his love, and that there is no story worth telling that cannot be improved on. He lives in Southeast Pennsylvania with his wife of forty years.